BENEATH THE CRIMSON SUN
A tale of revolution and retribution

RANZZITH CHAVA

BLUEROSE PUBLISHERS
India | U.K.

Copyright © Ranzzith Chava 2024

All rights reserved by author. No part of this publication may be reproduced, stored in a retrieval system or transmitted in any form or by any means, electronic, mechanical, photocopying, recording or otherwise, without the prior permission of the author. Although every precaution has been taken to verify the accuracy of the information contained herein, the publisher assumes no responsibility for any errors or omissions. No liability is assumed for damages that may result from the use of information contained within.

BlueRose Publishers takes no responsibility for any damages, losses, or liabilities that may arise from the use or misuse of the information, products, or services provided in this publication.

For permissions requests or inquiries regarding this publication, please contact:

BLUEROSE PUBLISHERS
www.BlueRoseONE.com
info@bluerosepublishers.com
+91 8882 898 898
+4407342408967

ISBN: 978-93-5989-815-5

Cover Design: Sadhna Kumari
Typesetting: Pooja Sharma

First Edition: March 2024

Dedicated to:

The the holy feet of the Divine Mother and the Master.

Each and every word of this narrative is the grace of the Divine Mother and Master.

Preface

In the fine fabric of history, there are narratives that transcend time, weaving together the threads of courage, resilience, and the indomitable spirit of those who dared to challenge the status quo. The tale that unfolds within these pages is one such saga—an odyssey of Rajini Kantha Reddy, a fictional Telugu Socialist (pre communist) activist who, in the British colonial India, stood as a beacon against the dark forces of fascism.

As we board on this journey, it is essential to acknowledge the inspiration drawn from countless real-life heroes who fought against oppression, echoing the struggles of individuals who sought justice in the face of tyranny. Rajini Reddy emerges from the creative realm, yet his story mirrors the collective spirit of those who have battled for equality and liberation throughout history.

The narrative unfolds in the rich tapestry of 19th-century India, where the echoes of oppression and the struggle for independence resonate. Rajini, a staunch communist, becomes a harbinger of change, standing tall against the forces that sought to subjugate the voice of the people. Through the pages that follow, we witness his evolution from a determined student to a relentless activist, navigating the complex terrain of societal upheaval and political turmoil.

This tale is not only a homage to the resilience of the human spirit but also an exploration of the complexities that define the struggle for justice. Rajini's journey is intertwined with the destinies of those who cross his path—Parvathi, Yadagiri, Varada Chary, and others, each contributing to the narrative tapestry with their dreams, sacrifices, and unwavering commitment to a cause larger than themselves.

The canvas of Rajini Reddy's life is painted with strokes of tragedy, triumph, and the relentless pursuit of a utopian vision. From the quaint villages of Telugu land to the bustling streets of colonial-era India, our protagonist transcends boundaries, embodying the universal quest for freedom and equality.

As we immerse ourselves in this narrative, let us be reminded that the echoes of Rajini's struggle reverberate far beyond the confines of fiction. They serve as a testament to the resilience of the human spirit, the pursuit of justice, and the unwavering belief that, even in the face of seemingly insurmountable odds, the flame of hope can illuminate the darkest corners of oppression.

May this tale inspire, provoke thought, and ignite the spark of change within each reader. For in the Rajini Reddy's fictional journey, we find reflections of the countless unsung heroes who, throughout history, have dared to challenge the shadows and pave the way for a brighter, more just tomorrow.

The Author

Ranzzith Chava

Introduction

In the heart of the British India, where the echoes of colonial dominance and feudal oppression reverberated through the fabric of society, emerged a figure whose journey would come to symbolize the relentless pursuit of justice and equality. Welcome to the world of Rajini kantha Reddy, a Telugu socialist,nationalist and (pre communist) activist whose fictional biography unfolds against the backdrop of political upheaval, social injustice, and the indomitable spirit of resistance.

As we traverse the pages of this narrative, we find ourselves transported to an era where the sun-drenched landscapes of Telugu land conceal the shadows of tyranny. Rajini Reddy, a beacon amidst the encroaching darkness, emerges as the protagonist of a tale that transcends fiction to explore the universal themes of human struggle, sacrifice, and the unwavering quest for a more just society.

This tale unfurls in a society gripped by the dual forces of colonial rule and feudal oppression. Through the eyes of Rajini, we navigate the complexities of a world teetering on the cusp of transformation. His journey, though fictional, mirrors the aspirations, challenges, and triumphs of those who dared to stand against the tide of injustice.

Amidst the quaint villages, bustling marketplaces, and political hotbeds of 19th-century India, Rajini's narrative unfolds as a tapestry woven with the threads of tragedy, resilience, and the unwavering commitment to ideals larger than oneself. It is a story that encapsulates the human spirit's capacity to endure, evolve, and resist even in the face of seemingly insurmountable odds.

As readers start on this literary odyssey, they are invited to witness Rajini's evolution—from a determined student grappling with societal inequalities to a fervent activist challenging the very foundations of a system built on exploitation. His companions—Parvathi, Yadagiri, Varada Chary—each bring their own dreams, struggles, and sacrifices, enriching the narrative tapestry with their individual stories.

Beyond the realm of fiction, Rajini's journey beckons readers to contemplate the universal struggle for justice, freedom, and societal transformation. The narrative is a mirror reflecting the echoes of countless historical struggles, inviting readers to explore the complexities of a society in flux and the individuals who, against all odds, sought to reshape its destiny.

Join us as we navigate the tumultuous waters of Rajini Reddy's life—a life woven into the intricate fabric of history, reminding us that even in the darkest corners, the flame of hope and resistance can illuminate the path toward a brighter, more equitable future.

Ranzzith Chava

Acknowledgment

To my Father, an activist himself, and my Mother, a catalyst of the activist, thank you for instilling in me the values that resonate within these pages. I am profoundly grateful for your love.

To my spouse and children: Your patience, understanding, and sacrifices have been the cornerstone of this literary journey. Your belief in me has been the wind in my sails, propelling me forward when the seas were rough. Thank you for being the silent muses that guided the words onto the page.

To my sister, who has been companion in both joy and challenge. Thank you for being a constant source of support and for sharing in the excitement.

To my mentors and friends whose encouragement and enthusiasm have created a ripple effect of positivity, I extend my deepest gratitude.

With heartfelt gratitude and appreciation,

Ranzzith Chava

Contents

Chapter 1: A Meal for All 1

Chapter 2: Where It All Started? 6

Chapter 3: Weaving the Web 11

Chapter 4: Scrambling the Web 16

Chapter 5: The Turning Point 21

Chapter 6: The Journey Begins 26

Chapter 7: Economic Drain 31

Chapter 8: The Secret Meeting – A Great Escape 36

Chapter 9: Rattled Dreams 41

Chapter 10: Homeward Bound: Rajini's Journey on the Montgomery 44

Chapter 11: A Changed Vision 47

Chapter 12: The Awakening 55

Chapter 13: A Journey beyond Social Boundaries 61

Chapter 14: The Resistance 68

Chapter 15: Heart Wrenching 71

Chapter 16: Somi – The oppressor 74

Chapter 17: The Rebellion 81

Chapter 18: The Village of Unity 85

Chapter 19: The Weavers' Weave of Resistance 90

Chapter 20: A Movement Is Born 97

Chapter 21: A Battle for Education 100
Chapter 22: The Inevitable 103
Chapter 23: A Promise Made 107
Chapter 24: The Feudal - British Alliance 112
Chapter 25: Flares and Smoke 116
Chapter 26: The Shock Waves 120
Chapter 27: Rajini Comes Home After the Release 124
Chapter 28: Rowlatt Act & Plan to Go Beyond 127
Chapter 29: The Battle Intensifies 133
Chapter 30: Call of Action 139
Chapter 31: Mentoring 145
Chapter 32: Plans for Uprising 153
Chapter 33: Missing 157
Chapter 34: Sri Aurobindo - The Vision of Future 164
Chapter 35: The Betrayal 169
Chapter 36: The Legacy Lives On 175

Chapter 1
A Meal for All

In the year 2000 as the mid-day sun beat down relentlessly and in "Muthyala Nagaram", a small telugu town in the coastal region of Southern part of India, a towering bronze statue in the junction of the town seemed glowing like a gold one in the light of the sun. Beside the statue is a very big neem tree which is an unofficial bus stop for the six trips of bus which takes the people to nearby villages and towns. A small crowd slowly started gathering under the shade of a big Neem tree. Next to the neem tree is a small mud hut. The hut with its thatched roof and the wooden supports eaten by termites is still a happening place. The place is filled all over with aroma of assured delicious food as the smoke goes out of the small old fashioned mud hut.

Two people came out of the hut and spread mats prepared from the leaves of wild palm trees. An oldman with a big moustache and beard interwoven, dressed in the traditional south Indian attire chopped onions and coriander in the hut, which is his "Annapurna" – A free meal centre (a non profitable hotel). His serene wrinkled face has a divine glow, he is very active even in his nineties. Wiping beads of sweat from his brow, he checked the bubbling pots of dal and rice one last time before ringing the old-fashioned bell, calling out that lunch is ready. Within minutes, the sparse courtyard filled with hungry farmers, labourers and travellers. There are beggars even in the line to have food, as hunger is so honest which knows no discrimination.

He smiled as he ladled steaming helpings of food onto banana leaves, his aged bones aching but his spirit uplifted by the appreciation in people's eyes. At just 50 paise a meal, his centre ensured no one in the village went hungry. The people drop the money into a pot held next to a serving pot with a satisfied, grateful expression after having their desired quantity of food. Some of the people volunteer up themselves to clean the place, the utensils and help the oldman for the next meal. But no one bothered about the ready to fall mud hut except the oldman, once in a while he tries himself to set the wood right and repair the thatched roof. It had been his life's work to carry on the charitable vision of his late father and his mentor. Looking out at the crowd, he spotted a school bus pull up.

A gaggle of chatty college students spilled out, chattering excitedly. "Appa, this place might have the best food for miles," said one girl, inhaling the aromatic scents deep into her lungs.

Her friend glanced at the towering statue at the centre's entrance. "Who is that man depicted? And why is his statue here?" she asked curiously.

Curiosity sparked among the students, and they began to inquire about the enigmatic figure immortalized in bronze. Students gathered around the statue, their faces filled with fascination. "Let's ask Rajesh, he might know, as his village is very near to this one", said a boy.

"Come on! Rajesh doesn't know about his own relatives in his village, how would you expect him to know", mocked a girl. Rajesh too started smiling along with others. Just then they heard some one say "Do you want to know about the statue? You will sure know but only after you have the meal."

The students turned to the direction from where the voice came and saw the old man with a glowing smiling face. The students readily agreed. He smiled gently as memories of his past flooded his mind. Come, let's eat first before I share his remarkable story." The students eagerly filled their leaves, digging in. Once all had eaten their fill, the oldman beckoned them to sit closer. The oldman, his face etched with the wisdom of years, stepped forward, ready to share the story in bits and pieces. The oldman started speaking, his voice filled with reverence.

In the statue's shadow, he began...

"That, my young friends, is Rajini Kantha Reddy. A name that echoes through the years of our history."

The students leaned in; their curiosity piqued by the Oldman's words. As the students settled around him expectantly, he closed his eyes and let his mind drift back in time.

"It was in the late 1800s when our village was under the cruel rule of the landlords, who taxed us mercilessly for every harvest. No one dared raise their voice in protest, for fear of harsh punishment. But there was a young man, he was different. He saw the injustice and was deeply pained by the poverty all around him. He rose like a Crimson Sun against the darkness of oppression and feudalism. Rajini Kantha Reddy, a skillful Kalari martial artist, an influential orator moreover a man with a golden heart and nerves of steel." The Oldman continuing the narrative, "Rajini was a visionary, a leader who once called this town home, which was then a village. He dedicated his life to the principles of justice, equality, and social transformation."

He described how Rajini Reddy's family, though affluent, renounced their wealth after witnessing peasants dying of starvation and ill treatment by the oppressors. The family began providing free education and medical aid, using his inheritance for the village's upliftment. "Rajini believed in the power of education, unity, and empathy. He led the villagers in their struggle for a more just and equitable society", the old man spoke very passionately.

"Naturally, this disturbed the landlords. They tried to silence Rajini, even imprisoning him a few times. But he emerged with his resolve strengthened. He traveled extensively, spreading his message of equal rights and dignity for all. Wherever he went, crowds gathered spellbound by his charismatic words."

The oldman's eyes shone as he recounted memorable speeches Reddy delivered. "He spoke of a just society where the poor need not fear or beg. His compassion gave people hope and urge to better their lives. Soon, protests erupted demanding fair wages, return of seized lands, and no increased taxes."

The agitation rattled the oppressors. He worked tirelessly to strengthen the unity between communities and castes. The landlords unleashed thugs to disrupt rallies but Reddy's calm mindset yet aggressive leadership gave tight slaps to the goons and feudals time and again. This left the goons confused and embarrassed.

As the years passed, more and more joined the movement each day. He paused as the students listened spellbound. In his mind's eye, he could visualise Rajini's fearless figure rallying thousands with his rousing words of change. The sketch he painted portrayed a man of vision and compassion, who awoke a village with his message of equality and justice. The Oldman sharing anecdotes. (Smiling) "We remember him for his bravery, his compassion, and his unwavering commitment to transforming lives. He was a beacon of hope."

The students listened with rapt attention, absorbing the essence of story of a man who had left an indelible mark on this community. In that moment, the students and the Oldman stood together, bridging the gap between generations, connected by the timeless tale of a man who had once called their village home – Rajini Kantha Reddy "The Red Flame of Revolution."

Chapter 2
Where It All Started?.......

One of the enthusiastic boys asked "What is your name thatha?"

"How old are you?" asked the other.

A boy stood and said, "Thatha, we want to know the entire story. Where it all started?"

The old man just smiled and said "Where it all started?"

He started the narration.

It was a Sunday during harvest season in the year 1900. The sun rose over the grain laden fields, casting its golden rays over the small village of Muthyalapuram, a modest village nestled in the lush hills of Madras Presidency, British India (now this town Muthyala Nagaram) . Young Rajini Kantha Reddy woke to the sounds of birds chirping outside his modest medieval house. Though his family now lived in poverty, they found joy in simple moments like these.

At 15 years old, Rajini was on the cusp of manhood. He helped his father Prakash Reddy tend to their small farm, while his mother Lakshmi cooked meals over an open fire. The Reddy family belonged to wealthy upper caste, yet they were looked down upon by their caste people as Prakash Reddy had socialistic views. He donated and spent most of his wealth for the betterment of the oppressed and down-trodden people. Rajini's parents raised him to value honesty, compassion, equality and the dignity of all human beings. From an early age, he was imbued with a strong sense of justice and an unquenchable thirst for knowledge.

One day, Rajini was returning home from the fields when he heard a commotion in the village square. To his shock, he saw his father and other men from the lower castes being publicly whipped and humiliated by henchmen of the local feudal lord Somi Reddy. When Rajini tried to stop the brutality, he was shoved to the ground and warned never to interfere again.

That night, Prakash Reddy explained to Rajini that the people were treated no more than slaves under Somi Reddy's authoritarian rule. Though the practice of untouchability had been discouraged by the most of the society, some of the upper caste people continued to treat them as filth. Rajini struggled to reconcile his father's words with his deeply held beliefs in justice and equality.

At 18, Rajini married Parvathi, his childhood love interest. Parvathi's gentleness and idealism complemented Rajini's fiery passion.

One of the boys interrupted, " A love marriage!"

"A love marriage in that era!", wondered a girl.

"Thatha, please narrate us their love story", two boys requested.

The oldman laughed and said "Okay, but I will narrate about their marriage first and as the story progresses, I will narrate their love story. The story of the marriage as narrated by my father to me."

"The Union of Hearts."

The marriage ceremony took place in our picturesque village nestled between rolling hills and lush fields. The backdrop of natural beauty added a touch of serenity to the proceedings. A rustic, open-air mandap (wedding canopy) was adorned with vibrant flowers and traditional decorations.

Rajini and Parvathi were both dressed in traditional attire. Rajini wore a meticulously tailored kurta and dhoti, while Parvathi was resplendent in a saree adorned with intricate embroidery. Their attire was a reflection of their cultural roots and the importance of honoring tradition.

The ceremony was presided over by village elders and a priest, who conducted the traditional rituals that symbolized the union of two souls. The chanting of mantras and the sprinkling of holy water filled the air with a sense of spiritual sanctity.

The exchange of garlands between Rajini and Parvathi was a moment of pure joy. As they placed the floral garlands around each other's necks, their eyes locked, and their smiles conveyed the depth of their love and commitment.

The Saptapadi, or seven sacred steps, were a pivotal part of the ceremony. As Rajini and Parvathi took each step together, they made promises to one another, pledging their love, respect, and devotion. It was a solemn and heartfelt expression of their commitment.

The couple sought the blessings of their parents, who, with tears of joy, placed their hands on their children's heads. The elders' blessings were a symbol of their approval and support for the union. The wedding was followed by jubilant celebrations. Villagers, family members, and friends joined in the festivities. There was singing, dancing, and feasting, as the entire village came together to celebrate the union of two beloved individuals.

Rajini and Parvathi's marriage is the beginning of a new chapter in their lives. It was not just a union of two individuals but a merging of two hearts that beat in harmony. Their love story has to endure the test of time, and they were ready to face the future hand in hand.

Rajini and Parvathi's life together was one of partnership. They supported each other's dreams and aspirations, working together to bring about the change they both believed in. Their marriage was not just about their love for each other; it was about their love for their community and their commitment to building a more just and equitable society. Together, they became champions of social change and justice. The love that Rajini and Parvathi shared was not just a personal love story; it was a testament to the power of love in shaping the destiny of a community.

Their partnership became a source of inspiration for those around them, a reminder of the strength that love and unity could bring. Their marriage was not just a celebration of love; it was a commitment to a shared purpose and a shared destiny, one in which they would stand together to bring about the change they had always believed in."

The students were listening carefully, anticipating the love story to unleash.

The old man said "No interruption from here on" and continued:

"During this time, a massive famine struck the region. Somi Reddy's men continued forcibly collecting taxes from the starving farmers and workers. The gross inhumanity Rajini witnessed lit a spark within him - he could no longer stand by in silence.

Rajini began speaking out against the unjust class system and criticizing Somi's unethical rule. Over the months, many youths inspired by his bravery, gathered to hear him speak. This soon caught the attention of Somi himself. He started utilizing all the strategies of "ASHTA DIGBANDHANA".

"What is Ashtadigbandana thatha?" interrupted a boy.

Chapter 3
Weaving the Web

"Ashtadigbandana – a way to corner and target a person or an entity from all the 8 directions, so that the target is strangled" replied the oldman.

"Explain it in detail thata", curiously asked a spectacled girl Shwetha.

The oldman smiled and continued...

The eight steps taken by Somi to bring down Rajini and his group are:

1. Propaganda and Smear Campaigns: Somi Reddy initiated a propaganda campaign to tarnish Rajini's reputation. This included spreading false rumors, allegations, and distorted stories about Rajini in an attempt to discredit him in the eyes of the local community.

2. Economic Pressure: Somi Reddy used his influence to exert economic pressure on those who supported Rajini or his causes. He threatened to withdraw financial support or job opportunities from individuals who openly aligned themselves with Rajini.

3. Intimidation and Threats: Somi Reddy's henchmen engaged in acts of intimidation and threats against Rajini's supporters and even against Rajini himself. They made it clear that those who sided with Rajini could face dire consequences.

4. Co-opting Local Authorities: Somi Reddy, who had political and economic influence, used his connections to

manipulate or co-opt local authorities. This made it difficult for Rajini to garner support for his initiatives and provided Somi Reddy with a degree of protection.

5. Suppression of Information: Somi Reddy's influence extended to local media outlets. He pressured or bribed these sources to avoid reporting on Rajini's activities or to present them in a negative light. This information blackout hampered Rajini's ability to reach a wider audience.

6. Division Among Supporters: Somi Reddy exploited existing divisions within the community. He sowed discord among different groups that supported Rajini, causing internal conflicts and weakening their united front.

7. Counter-Propaganda: Somi Reddy's camp produced its own narrative to counter Rajini's message. They created stories and propaganda that sought to paint Somi Reddy as a benefactor of the community, undermining Rajini's claims of injustice.

8. Legal Harassment: Somi Reddy initiated legal actions against Rajini and his supporters, tying them up in time-consuming legal battles that drained resources and diverted their focus from their mission.

Somi Reddy's efforts to counter Rajini's growing popularity were a mix of manipulation, intimidation, and subversion. These tactics were aimed at undermining Rajini's influence and quashing the movement for justice and social change that Rajini was leading.

Out of all the strategies used by Somi in ashta digbandhana of Rajini's rise, Propaganda and threats were main weapons.

Propaganda and Smear Campaigns:

Somi Reddy's campaign to counter Rajini's growing popularity began with a calculated strategy of discrediting

Rajini through propaganda and smear campaigns. This involved spreading false information, rumors, and damaging allegations to tarnish Rajini's reputation and create doubt in the minds of the local community.

Creation of False Narratives: Somi Reddy's henchmen and propagandists concocted stories that portrayed Rajini in a negative light. These stories often included fabricated incidents or taken-out-of-context statements to create the impression that Rajini was involved in illegal and immoral activities.

Utilizing Local Gossip Networks: To ensure the spread of these false narratives, Somi Reddy's network leveraged existing local gossip channels and informal communication networks. They used word-of-mouth, small gatherings, and community meetings to disseminate the damaging stories about Rajini.

Demonization of Rajini: The propaganda aimed to depict Rajini as a divisive figure who was causing unrest in the community. They portrayed him as an outsider who was exploiting local issues for personal gain, rather than as a committed activist fighting for social justice.

Manipulation of Public Opinion: The goal was to manipulate public opinion and create doubts about Rajini's integrity and intentions. This could sway neutral or undecided community members away from supporting him and his causes.

Intimidation and Threats: Somi Reddy resorted to intimidation and threats as a means to silence and deter Rajini from his activism. This strategy involved various tactics aimed at creating fear, undermining Rajini's determination, and discouraging him from pursuing his social justice initiatives.

"How intimidation and threats were employed to bring down the lion thatha?" asked Swarup, son of a fisher man.

The old man laughed and said even lions can be pulled down by a pack of hyenas.

Some of Somi Reddy's henchmen confronted Rajini during a public gathering. They warned him that if he continued his activities, he and his family would face dire consequences.

Verbal threats aimed to create a climate of fear and insecurity, making Rajini think twice about his actions.

Rajini received anonymous threats through letters, posters and sometimes stone pelting, indicating that his safety and the safety of his family were at risk.

These threats were intended to put pressure on Rajini by making him feel physically vulnerable, compelling him to reconsider his activism.

Rajini noticed unknown individuals constantly monitoring his activities, both in public and at home.

Surveillance was a tactic to create paranoia and distress, with the aim of making Rajini believe that his every move was being closely observed.

Rajini's home and property were vandalized on multiple occasions. For example, his office was broken into, and important documents were tampered with and stolen.

Vandalism was meant to disrupt Rajini's work, damage his resources, and send a clear message that his efforts were unwelcome.

Some of Rajini's key supporters and collaborators received threats or were subjected to acts of intimidation, like their businesses being targeted.

By targeting those who stood by Rajini, Somi Reddy aimed to isolate him and weaken the network of support that sustained his activism.

False allegations and derogatory rumors about Rajini's personal life were spread in the community.

The intention was to tarnish Rajini's reputation and diminish his credibility as a leader, making people hesitant to align themselves with him.

Rajini faced a series of frivolous legal cases filed against him, requiring significant time and resources to address.

Legal harassment was intended to exhaust Rajini and his supporters, divert their focus, and weaken their resolve.

Some businesses owned by individuals close to Rajini suffered economic losses due to pressure from Somi Reddy's associates.

Economic retaliation sought to weaken Rajini's support base by affecting the livelihoods of his allies.

While Somi Reddy's intimidation and threat tactics created moments of fear and vulnerability, Rajini's unwavering commitment to the cause of social justice, his strong character, and the resilience of his supporters allowed him to persevere despite these challenges. Rajini's ability to stand firm in the face of threats and the indomitable spirit of his movement made him a super hero.

"Oh my God! How did the hero survive this horrible situation?", asked Sagar, son of a village head of a nearby village.

Chapter 4
Scrambling the Web

"**How?**" Smiled the oldman.

"The Resilience of Rajini's Character and the Unwavering Faith of the People helped him survive these tough situations.", proudly said the oldman.

Somi Reddy's smear campaign against Rajini was a strategic attempt to discredit him and tarnish his reputation in the eyes of the community. However, this campaign ultimately failed due to the unwavering faith the people had in Rajini and the strength of his character.

Rajini's character and the trust of the people played a pivotal role in the failure of the smear campaign. He had cultivated an impeccable reputation over the years. He was known for his unwavering commitment to social justice, his honesty, and his tireless efforts to improve the lives of the community members. His character was marked by integrity, compassion, and selflessness. This reputation had been built through years of consistent actions and was deeply ingrained in the community's consciousness. His actions spoke louder than any allegations or rumors. People had witnessed the positive changes he had brought about, from addressing local issues to advocating for their rights. This consistency in his commitment made it difficult for the smear campaign to hold ground.

He had formed deep and personal connections with the people he served. He knew their names, their families, and their struggles. He was accessible and approachable, always willing to listen to their concerns. These personal connections created a bond of trust that was not easily eroded by external propaganda. The people in the community were not passive observers; they were active participants in Rajini's journey. Many had directly benefited from his initiatives and witnessed the positive changes he had brought about. They shared stories and testimonials of their experiences, countering the smear campaign with real-life examples of Rajini's impact.

Rajini consistently held the moral high ground. He never engaged in personal attacks or responded to the smear campaign with negativity. His focus remained on his mission for social justice and the welfare of the community. This principled approach resonated with the people and further solidified their trust in him. His unwavering commitment to his cause was exemplified by his resilience in the face of adversity.

He continued to work for social justice, even in the midst of the smear campaign. The people admired his steadfastness and determination, which further endeared him to them. The community had a deep emotional connection with Rajini. He was not just a leader but a beloved member of the community. This emotional bond made it particularly challenging for the smear campaign to break the trust between Rajini and the people.

One of the key reasons why Somi Reddy's plans failed was the deep and personal connections that Rajini had formed with the people he served. These connections were not merely superficial; they were built on trust, mutual respect, and a genuine commitment to the well-being of the community.

"I didn't quite seem to understand, please tell some examples thatha", said a boy named Manoj.

The oldman nodded and continued....

Accessible and Approachable: Rajini made it a point to be highly accessible and approachable to the community members. He attended local gatherings, community meetings, and social events, where he listened to their concerns and issues. He was often seen walking through the villages, engaging in conversations with people, and visiting their homes.

*Rajini regularly visited the homes of elderly community members to inquire about their well-being. He would spend time talking with them, offering assistance, and sometimes even running errands on their behalf. This level of personal interaction created a strong bond of trust.

Knowing the People: Rajini knew the people he served not just by name but also by their family backgrounds, their stories, and their struggles. He remembered their children's names, their aspirations, and their challenges. This personal knowledge showed that he genuinely cared about the individuals in the community.

*When a family in the community faced a crisis, Rajini not only provided assistance but also took the time to understand the root causes of their difficulties. This personalized approach ensured that his help was effective and relevant to their specific needs.

Immediate Responses: Whenever an issue or concern arose in the community, Rajini responded promptly. He made himself available to address urgent matters and provided practical solutions. This responsiveness increased the community's confidence in his leadership.

*When a village faced a sudden water shortage due to a broken well, Rajini coordinated a quick response. He mobilized resources, arranged for the repair of the well, and ensured that clean water was available to the villagers within a matter of days. This immediate response demonstrated his dedication.

Approachable Listening Sessions: Rajini organized regular community listening sessions where people could openly voice their opinions, grievances, and suggestions. He patiently listened to their feedback and made efforts to incorporate their ideas into his initiatives.

*During one of these sessions, a group of young adults expressed their desire for vocational training to improve their employment prospects. Rajini not only acknowledged their request but also arranged some cross training sessions for skill development programs, enabling them to gain new skills and find better job opportunities.

These examples illustrate how Rajini's personal connections were based on genuine engagement, empathy, and a willingness to go the extra mile to support the community. These connections created a bond of trust that was not easily broken, as the people saw Rajini not just as a leader but as a friend and advocate who was deeply invested in their well-being. This level of trust made it challenging for any smear campaign to undermine their faith in him. In the end, the smear campaign's failure could be attributed to the fact that character and trust are not easily undermined by baseless allegations and rumors. The people had seen Rajini's actions and dedication firsthand, and their unwavering faith in him was unshakable. This was a must to the enduring power of a leader with an unassailable character and a community that believed in the principles he stood for.

As none of his strategies worked, the frustrated feudal lord took some extreme steps to teach Rajini a lesson and quiet him up permanently.

One evening, his henchmen dragged Rajini's parents from their house, hit them mercilessly and brutally murdered them in front of the entire village. A clear warning to Rajini - cease his dissent, or face dire consequences.

Rajini, a Kalari expert himself, in his agony, raged with the death of his parents took a hammer and a sickle to get his revenge. Parvathi pleaded Rajini to stop his crusade, for the sake of their newly born daughter Lakshmi. But he refused to be silenced. He went out and thrashed the goons who killed his parents. Some of the goons became limbless and some have their life critical. Somi, whose ego now got hurt deeply with unexpected retaliation from Rajini is waiting for the right moment like a coiled snake to strike back. Rajini made his point clear to Parvathi - "As long as oppression exists, my struggle will continue." With a heavy heart, she decided to stand by him no matter whatever the cost.

Chapter 5
The Turning Point

It was a scorching summer day when a young Rajini Kantha, barely 20 years old, stood at the forefront of a protest in front of the British Viceroy's residence. The cause was just - they were demanding justice against the tyrannical actions of a local feudal lord, Somi Reddy, who had been terrorizing the villagers for far too long.

Rajini Reddy was a commanding figure just at 20, standing at an impressive 6 feet tall. His presence alone could fill a room, and his striking appearance made him a natural leader. He had a strong, well-built frame that conveyed both physical strength and resilience.

His skin was a warm, sun-kissed brown, a symbol of his life in rural India. Rajini's expressive face was adorned with a neatly trimmed beard that framed his square jawline, giving him an air of authority. His deep-set eyes were a piercing shade of brown, often reflecting a profound intensity and determination.

Rajini's hair was raven-black and neatly combed, though the weight of his responsibilities sometimes caused a few strands to fall rebelliously across his forehead. He typically wore simple, traditional clothing – a khadi kurta (a long, loose-fitting shirt) and dhoti, symbolizing his commitment to the Indian way of life and his connection to the common people.

His voice, when he spoke, was both powerful and soothing, carrying the weight of wisdom and conviction. His eyes, though intense, were also capable of conveying empathy and understanding, endearing him to those who followed him.

The protest area where Rajini Reddy led the rally against the injustices perpetrated by Somi Reddy and the British colonial authorities was a dynamic tableau of fervent activism and determination. The protest took place in a spacious and dusty clearing near the heart of the village. Surrounded by ancient, gnarled trees that offered patches of welcome shade, the clearing provided a natural amphitheater where villagers could assemble.

On that day, the area was densely packed with villagers of all ages, backgrounds, and social statuses. Men, women, and children gathered with a shared sense of purpose, their faces etched with determination and hope. The atmosphere was charged with anticipation.

The protesters held aloft handmade banners and placards that bore slogans demanding justice and condemning the oppressive actions of Somi Reddy and the British colonial authorities. These colorful banners swayed in the breeze, their messages a powerful visual representation of the people's resolve.

At the center of the clearing, a makeshift stage had been erected from wooden crates and old boards. It served as the platform from which Rajini Reddy delivered his impassioned speeches.

The air was filled with the rhythmic chants and songs of the protesters, their voices rising in unison as they expressed their collective anger and determination. The cadence of these chants echoed through the clearing, reverberating with a sense of unity and purpose.

Along the periphery of the protest area, British colonial police officers stood watch, their stern faces a stark contrast to the passionate assembly. They were armed with batons and rifles, a constant reminder of the potential for confrontation.

The protest area was not just a physical space; it was a crucible of emotions. Anger, hope, and frustration mingled in the air, creating an atmosphere charged with the energy of change. The area bore witness to the resilience of a people who had chosen to stand up against oppression and fight for their rights.

The British colonial police, backed by Somi Reddy's menacing henchmen, attempted to dismantle the crowd and disperse the protest. But they hadn't anticipated the unwavering determination and meticulous planning behind this protest. Rajini Kantha, with his fiery speeches and unyielding spirit, had rallied the villagers into a disciplined and united force.

The protesters stood their ground, chanting slogans for justice and holding aloft placards that told the harrowing stories of Somi Reddy's atrocities. The police's batons and threats were met with a sea of resolute faces.

As the chaos unfolded, an English businessman, who had recently arrived to establish a factory nearby, found himself drawn to the commotion. His initial curiosity soon turned into admiration as he observed the exceptional leadership and administrative skills displayed by young Rajini Kantha.

The English businessman, whose name was Frederick Hartman, watched in awe as Rajini Kantha efficiently organized the protesters, maintained discipline, and kept their morale high. He couldn't help but be impressed by this young Indian leader who was fearlessly challenging the British colonial authorities and a powerful local landlord.

Hartman was not just impressed; he was deeply moved. He saw in Rajini Kantha the potential for real change in the region, not just in terms of political freedom but also in terms of socio-economic transformation.

Frederick Hartman, was a distinguished figure in his late 40s who possessed an air of worldly sophistication and gravitas. His presence exuded a sense of authority and confidence that had been honed through years of international business dealings. He stood at an average height, with a well-proportioned build that spoke of a life of comfort and affluence. His frame was neither imposing nor diminutive but carried a distinct air of refinement.

He sported neatly combed silver hair that framed his face in a distinguished manner. His hair, while showing the wisdom of age, was impeccably groomed, reflecting his meticulous attention to detail. Hartman possessed a square jawline that added a touch of strength to his appearance. His facial features were sharp, including a well-defined nose and piercing blue eyes that hinted at an astute and perceptive nature. Crow's feet at the corners of his eyes hinted at a lifetime of experiences and wisdom.

He was often seen in tailored suits that exuded English elegance, a sartorial choice that reflected his status as a successful businessman. His choice of attire was always impeccable, showcasing his penchant for refinement and professionalism.

Frederick Hartman's demeanor was characterized by a blend of suaveness and gravitas. He had a confident, yet not overbearing, manner of speaking that commanded attention. His refined gestures and calm composure revealed a man who was accustomed to navigating complex negotiations and high-stakes business dealings.

Hartman's expression was typically one of thoughtful contemplation, and his eyes held a hint of curiosity and open-mindedness. While he exuded an air of authority, he was also known for his approachability and willingness to engage in meaningful conversations.

His interactions with the Indian community reflected a deep respect for the local culture and traditions. Hartman's genuine interest in understanding and contributing to the betterment of the region endeared him to the local population.

Despite his success as a businessman, Hartman's encounter with Rajini Reddy and the protest had sparked in him a desire to become more than just a profiteer. It had ignited a passion for social justice and had set him on a path of collaboration with Rajini, ultimately leading to a life-changing partnership for both of them.

After the protest ended, Hartman approached Rajini Kantha and offered his support. He saw an opportunity to not only invest in his factory but also to contribute to the betterment of the local community. Rajini Kantha, always open to alliances that could benefit his people, accepted Hartman's offer cautiously.

Over time, a unique bond formed between the two men. They worked together to improve the conditions of the local villagers, providing employment opportunities, healthcare, and education. Hartman, who had once come to India as a businessman, became an advocate for social justice with Rajini Kantha's guidance.

In Rajini Kantha, Hartman had found not just a leader but a brother, a comrade in the battle for justice, and an inspiration for his own transformation from a businessman seeking profit to a champion of social change. Their bond would go on to shape the destiny of the region, as they worked together to create a legacy of progress, unity, and justice that would be remembered for generations to come.

Chapter 6
The Journey Begins

Soon after, a fortuitous opportunity arose for Rajini. Hartman offered to sponsor his studies abroad. Understanding that global education could take the revolution to next level, Rajini accepted the offer. He made sure that Parvathi's parents are with her. At the age of 21, with the support of Hartman, with wishes from his wife and infant daughter's, Rajini left for England. There he hoped to gain new knowledge and skills before returning home to continue his fight for justice.

As the day of departure neared, Rajini Reddy's heart raced with a heady mix of excitement and trepidation. The opportunity to travel to England for education, sponsored by Frederick Hartman, was a dream come true. The bustling railway station in the nearby town buzzed with activity as travelers bid farewell to their loved ones.

Rajini was dressed in his finest attire, a well-pressed khadi kurta and dhoti, symbolizing his Indian identity and his commitment to his roots. Over his shoulder, he carried a leather satchel that held the few belongings he would need for the journey.

His eyes sparkled with anticipation, and a determined smile played on his lips. He was acutely aware of the weight of the expectations placed upon him by his community and his own aspirations to bring about change.

At the station, friends, family members, and well-wishers had gathered to bid him farewell. His parents, their eyes brimming with pride and sorrow, bestowed blessings upon him. The village elders offered sage advice, reminding him of the importance of preserving his culture and values abroad.

The rhythmic chug of the steam engine and the hiss of escaping steam signaled the arrival of the train. Rajini climbed aboard, and the crowd on the platform cheered, waving colorful scarves and handkerchiefs.

The Transcontinental Journey was a transcontinental odyssey that would take him from the heart of rural India to the culturally rich cities of England. The train clattered along the tracks, taking him away from the familiar sights and sounds of his homeland.

The train passed through diverse landscapes, from lush green fields and dense forests to bustling towns and serene villages. The ever-changing scenery outside the window was a visual symphony of nature's beauty.

Inside the train compartment, Rajini shared space with a diverse group of fellow travelers. He struck up conversations with some of them, exchanging stories and perspectives. Their cultural diversity fascinated him, and he absorbed each encounter as a learning opportunity.

As the train journeyed through different regions, Rajini encountered a kaleidoscope of languages and dialects. It was a reminder of the linguistic diversity of India, which he would carry with him to England.

After several days and nights of travel via train and ship, Rajini arrived at the city where he would pursue his education. The bustling city square was a stark contrast to the tranquil villages of India.

The cityscape was a captivating blend of architectural marvels, with grand buildings and cobblestone streets that bore witness to centuries of history. The sights and sounds of London were a sensory overload for Rajini.

Waiting at the square was Frederick Hartman, his face lit up with a warm smile. The reunion was filled with a sense of gratitude and camaraderie. Hartman, fluent in several languages, ensured that Rajini felt welcomed and at ease.

Over the following days, Rajini settled into his new life in England. He navigated the intricacies of his educational institution, where he was met with a rigorous academic curriculum. Hartman provided guidance and support, ensuring that Rajini had everything he needed to excel.

Rajini described London in his diary :

In the early 1900s, London retained much of its historical charm while also embracing modern developments, creating a cityscape that exuded a unique beauty and character:

London's skyline was marked by architectural marvels. St. Paul's Cathedral, with its iconic dome, stood as a timeless symbol of the city's history. The Houses of Parliament along the River Thames and the Tower Bridge, a magnificent feat of Victorian engineering, added to the city's beauty.

London was adorned with beautifully landscaped parks and gardens. Hyde Park, Kensington Gardens, Regent's Park, and St. James's Park provided serene retreats amidst the bustling city, featuring lush greenery, picturesque lakes, and elegant pathways. The city was steeped in history, boasting landmarks such as the Tower of London, with its medieval architecture and storied past. The British Museum, housing priceless artifacts from across the globe, was a testament to the city's cultural richness.

Much of London's beauty stemmed from its Victorian-era architecture. Rows of elegant townhouses, Georgian squares, and ornate terraces showcased intricate facades, decorative details, and stately interiors, adding to the city's visual allure.

London was a cultural hub, with theaters, opera houses, and galleries that epitomized artistic excellence. The West End theaters, including the Royal Opera House and the Globe Theatre, offered a vibrant mix of performances and entertainment.

The River Thames served as a centerpiece, offering scenic views of iconic landmarks and bustling activity. Riverside promenades, lined with cafes and promenades, provided picturesque vistas of London's bridges and historic buildings.

The city at night was a spectacle, with gas-lit streets casting a warm glow on cobblestone alleys and historic lanes. The ambiance created an enchanting atmosphere, reminiscent of an era marked by old-world charm.

London's markets, such as Covent Garden and Borough Market, were vibrant hubs of activity. The shopping districts of Oxford Street and Bond Street showcased a blend of modern commerce within a historical setting. Horse-drawn carriages traversed the streets, adding a touch of elegance to London's transportation. The introduction of electric trams and the city's underground railway system added to the allure of its evolving transportation landscape.

Throughout the year, London's beauty transformed with the seasons. From the vibrant blooms of spring in its parks to the wintertime charm of snowy streets and festive decorations, each season brought a unique and captivating allure to the city.

London in the early 1900s was a city that seamlessly blended its rich history, cultural heritage, and architectural splendor with the advancements of a rapidly evolving modern era, creating a tapestry of beauty that captivated residents and visitors alike.

The Academic Environment: Rajini was immersed in an intellectually stimulating environment, surrounded by students from around the world. He attended lectures, engaged in spirited debates, and absorbed the knowledge that would fuel his future endeavors.

Chapter 7
Economic Drain

As Rajini embarked on his educational journey in London, he was acutely aware of the responsibility that came with this opportunity. He understood that his purpose extended beyond personal growth; it was about gaining the knowledge and skills needed to effect meaningful change in his homeland.

Rajini's keen observation made him realise about the flow of wealth from British colonies to London, enriching the capital at the expense of the colonies, and astute understanding of the dynamics of colonial exploitation and economic imperialism prevalent during that time.

His comprehension includes several crucial aspects:

Economic Drain from Colonies: The colonies, under British rule, were exploited for their resources, labor, and wealth. The natural resources extracted from these colonies, including minerals, agricultural produce, and other commodities, were exploited for the benefit of the British Empire.

Imbalanced Trade Relationships: The trade policies established by the British favored London's interests. The colonies were often forced into one-sided trade relationships where they had to export raw materials at low prices and import finished goods at inflated rates from Britain, contributing to the economic subjugation of the colonies.

Capital Accumulation in London: The profits generated from this exploitative system flowed back to London, contributing significantly to the wealth and prosperity of the capital city. The capital accrued from colonial trade furthered industrialization, infrastructure development, and cultural advancements in London.

Economic Disparities and Colonies' Poverty: This systematic exploitation led to the impoverishment and underdevelopment of the colonies. The wealth drained from the colonies left them economically weakened, hindering their capacity for independent economic growth and social progress.

Colonial Resistance and Nationalist Movements: Understanding this exploitation fuelled Rajini's commitment to anti-colonial resistance and nationalist movements. He advocated for the economic emancipation of the colonies, calling for fair trade, self-determination, and the repatriation of resources to benefit the indigenous populations.

Rajini's recognition of this economic exploitation would likely strengthen his resolve in fighting against colonial oppression and advocating for equitable economic policies that aimed to rectify the imbalances created by colonialism. His understanding might also challenge the exploitative economic structures imposed by the British Empire.

Rajini maintained a regular correspondence with his family and community back in India. He shared his experiences, the knowledge he acquired, and his unwavering commitment to their cause. His letters were a source of inspiration for those eagerly awaiting his return.

Letter to Ravi:

Rajini's letter to his friend Ravi, outlining his detailed understanding of the economic exploitation of colonies and how it enriches London:

Dear Ravi,

I hope this letter finds you in good health. I've been reflecting deeply on the economic conditions prevailing in our colonies and the intricacies of the financial dynamics between our homeland and the capital city of London.

One of the fundamental realizations that has struck me profoundly is the manner in which the economic structure, primarily orchestrated by the British, siphons off the wealth from our colonies, channeling it directly to London. This channeling of wealth seems to follow a consistent pattern – a pattern that perpetuates the impoverishment of our colonies while bolstering the affluence of the metropolis.

As we delve into this matter further. The trade relationships enforced by the colonial powers exhibit a clear imbalance. The commodities and raw materials harvested from our lands, often at the cost of immense toil and sacrifice by our people, are systematically exported to London.

However, the prices fetched for these resources are kept artificially low, unjustly undervaluing the immense worth of our produce.

Conversely, the finished goods and manufactured products originating from London are then forced back into our colonies, but these goods arrive with exorbitant price tags. The inflated rates imposed on these imports drain our resources further, creating a cycle where our people remain deprived of the fruits of their labor.

This economic drain contributes significantly to the accumulation of wealth in London. The profits amassed from this exploitative system flow back to the capital, fueling its industrial advancements, infrastructure development, and cultural endeavors. Meanwhile, the very colonies that sustain this economic engine are left struggling, their economies stunted, and their people marginalized.

This stark disparity in economic fortune has become painfully evident to me. It fuels my determination to challenge the colonial structures and advocate for fair trade, self-determination, and the rightful repatriation of resources to our colonies. I firmly believe that rectifying these economic imbalances is crucial to fostering genuine progress, dignity, and prosperity for our people.

Take good care of yourself.

Yours in solidarity,

Rajini

Cultural Exploration: In his free time, Rajini explored the city, taking in its art, music, and cultural diversity. He visited museums, attended concerts, and savored the flavors of English cuisine, all of which broadened his horizons.

Over the next few years, Rajini was exposed to a myriad of new radical ideas that expanded his worldview. He met thinkers, activists and fellow students from Africa, China, and Russia. He read the works of Voltaire, Thomas Paine and other philosophers. But most influentially, he discovered the writings of the German philosophers **Karl Marx** and **Friedrich Engels**. Marx's critique of capitalism and class struggle resonated deeply in Rajini. He saw now that the poor plight of India's stemmed from its colonial rule under the British crown. Only a revolution led by the working class could break the chains of their servitude. As he soaked in Marxist theories, Rajini came to view himself as part of a larger global struggle against imperial power structures.

The small village uprisings he had led were ripples connected to a larger wave sweeping across continents.

Chapter 8
The Secret Meeting – A Great Escape

"*Only a revolution led by the working class could break the chains of their servitude*"

Rajini's commitment to serving the motherland was a flame that burned brightly within him, ignited by a deep sense of responsibility and a yearning for India's freedom from colonial oppression. From a young age, he had witnessed the injustices and hardships faced by his fellow countrymen under British rule, and this ignited a passionate determination within him to contribute to the cause of liberation. The determination to serve the motherland was a fervent and deeply rooted aspect of Rajini's character, driving him to join secret societies like **"Lotus and Dagger,"** inspired by the spirit of patriotism and a desire for India's liberation.

As he joined the secret society **"Lotus and Dagger,"** he found a fraternity of like-minded individuals who shared his fervor for India's independence. Learning about the society's previous members, including the revered Sri Aurobindo Ghose, further fueled Rajini's sense of purpose. He admired Ghose's dedication and vision for a free and self-reliant India, finding inspiration in his ideologies and actions.

He was driven by an unwavering belief in the potential of his homeland. He envisioned an India free from foreign subjugation, where every individual could thrive in a society built on justice, equality, and dignity. His hunger to serve the motherland was not just a fleeting sentiment but a guiding principle that shaped his choices, actions, and sacrifices.

His involvement in the secret society was not merely a clandestine endeavor; it was a commitment to the greater cause of India's emancipation. Rajini engaged in discussions, debates, and strategic planning sessions, channeling his intellect and passion to strategize ways to awaken national consciousness and mobilize the masses for the struggle ahead. Rajini's will to serve the motherland was not driven by personal ambition but by an altruistic desire to uplift his fellow countrymen. He envisioned a future where India would reclaim its sovereignty, cultural heritage, and self-governance.

In every action he took, every word he spoke, and every sacrifice he made, Rajini's dedication to the cause of India's liberation shone through. His hunger to serve the motherland became the guiding force that shaped his identity, forging a path of unwavering commitment, sacrifice, and unwavering patriotism. Rajini's passion to serve the motherland was an integral part of his being, propelling him to join secret societies and dedicate himself wholeheartedly to the struggle for India's freedom. This hunger fueled his determination to withstand any challenges or sacrifices that lay ahead on the path to freedom.

In the shadows of secrecy and looming threat, the clandestine meeting of "Lotus and Dagger" was about to convene. Rajini, along with the society members, had meticulously planned this crucial gathering, aiming to discuss strategies for India's liberation from British rule.

However, their carefully guarded meeting was compromised by a tip-off to the British police.

As dusk descended, a squad of British officers, armed and determined, surrounded the premises where the meeting was underway. The sudden intrusion sent waves of tension and urgency among the society members. Rajini, quick-witted and composed even in the face of danger, swiftly sprang into action to ensure the safety of the members.

Amidst the chaos and commotion, Rajini acted decisively, leading the group through a predetermined escape route. With calm yet urgent instructions, he guided his fellow members through hidden passages and concealed exits, using the darkness to their advantage.

The members of "Lotus and Dagger," their hearts pounding with adrenaline, followed Rajini's lead, navigating the maze-like corridors and secret passageways of the building. They moved swiftly and silently, their breaths shallow as they evaded the encroaching threat of the British authorities.

Rajini's meticulous planning proved invaluable as they managed to evade the police dragnet without leaving a trace. Each member, masked by the cover of darkness, slipped away unnoticed, ensuring that their identities remained safeguarded and their mission undisclosed.

The escape was a solid proof of Rajini's leadership, quick thinking, and strategic prowess. His ability to remain composed under pressure and orchestrate a seamless getaway ensured the safety of all the society members, preventing any compromising information from falling into the hands of the authorities.

As the dawn broke and the chaos of the raid settled, the British police found themselves baffled by the empty premises. Despite their thorough search, they discovered no evidence, no names, and no clues that could unravel the clandestine activities of "Lotus and Dagger."

The society members dispersed quietly, their identities concealed, and their unity strengthened by the successful evasion. Rajini's brilliant escape plan had ensured that the spirit of "Lotus and Dagger" remained unbroken, shrouded in secrecy, ready to continue their fight for India's liberation from the shadows.

The Master's Speech

One day, Rajini received a letter from Ravi.

He opened the letter with a smile and started reading the letter enthusiastically.

This letter illustrates Ravi's heartfelt account of the transformative experience he had while attending Sri Aurobindo Ghose's inspirational speech, conveying the essence of the spiritual and patriotic fervor that swept through the audience.

Dear Rajini,

I trust this letter finds you in good health and high spirits. I cannot contain my excitement as I write to recount an experience that has left an indelible mark on my soul. I recently had the honor of attending Sri Aurobindo Ghose's powerful and transformative speech at Uttarpara.

The atmosphere was charged with an aura of anticipation as people from all walks of life gathered in the assembly. The air was thick with fervor and hope for our nation's destiny. As Sri Aurobindo took the stage, his presence commanded reverence and respect. His words, eloquent and impassioned, resonated with a wisdom that transcended the ordinary.

He began by invoking the spirit of nationalism, igniting a fervent sense of patriotism within every heart present. His vision for a free and resurgent India reverberated through his words, stirring a deep sense of purpose among the audience. Sri Aurobindo's call for India's liberation was not just a political aspiration but a spiritual awakening, a realization that our nation's destiny was intertwined with its spiritual and cultural heritage.

His speech delved into the essence of our nationhood, emphasizing the importance of self-reliance, cultural resurgence, and unity among our diverse communities. Sri Aurobindo eloquently articulated the need for a collective consciousness that transcends religious, linguistic, and regional boundaries, envisioning a united India standing tall in its diversity.

His words were not merely rhetoric; they were a beacon of hope, guiding us towards a future where every Indian would stand proud and free. Sri Aurobindo's vision was not limited to political independence alone; it encompassed the awakening of our collective consciousness, heralding a new era of spiritual and cultural renaissance.

The audience hung onto every word, spellbound by the depth of his vision and the intensity of his conviction. As he concluded his speech, the fervor and determination among the listeners were palpable. His words had ignited a flame of resolve within us, a commitment to contribute to the greater cause of India's emancipation.

Rajini, the impact of Sri Aurobindo's speech was profound, and I cannot help but feel invigorated and inspired by his vision. His message resonates deeply within me, echoing your own aspirations for our motherland's freedom and progress.

Be safe dear brother.

Yours trustworthy,

Ravi

Chapter 9
Rattled Dreams

Rajini's journey was far from over. England had provided him with invaluable knowledge and experiences, but his heart remained tethered to the villages of India. As the years passed, Rajini continued to grow, both as an individual and as a leader. His education in England had equipped him with the tools needed to effect change, and he was determined to return to India and make a difference. The journey, which had begun with a single train ride, had evolved into a lifelong pursuit of justice and transformation. And Rajini Reddy, armed with knowledge and driven by purpose, was ready to face the challenges that lay ahead, with the unwavering support of Frederick Hartman and the dreams of a better India guiding his path.

Hartman, Rajini's benefactor and a man who had supported his education in Europe, faced a tremendous setback when his shipping business suffered irreparable losses. The devastating storm wreaked havoc on his fleet of ships, causing financial ruin. Unable to withstand the crippling aftermath of the disaster, Hartman found himself drowning in insurmountable debts and hardships.

Rajini, unaware of the turmoil that had unfolded in Hartman's life, had departed for Dublin on an imperative meeting, focused on furthering his research. Little did he know of the tragedy that awaited his return.

Upon Rajini's homecoming, instead of a warm welcome, he was greeted by the heart-wrenching news of Hartman's demise. The weight of this unexpected loss, compounded by the abrupt revelation of Hartman's financial downfall and personal turmoil, shook Rajini to his core.

Learning of Hartman's wife leaving him in the aftermath of the business losses and the subsequent tragedy of his god-given brother taking his own life, Rajini was engulfed in grief and disbelief. He found himself standing amidst the wreckage of his mentor's life, grappling with the loss of someone who had been a guiding light in his journey.

In the wake of Hartman's tragic end, Rajini, feeling a deep sense of responsibility and indebtedness, took it upon himself to carry out the final rites and honor Hartman's memory. With a heavy heart and a soul burdened by sorrow, he sought the assistance of Chapman, the lawyer associated with Hartman's firm, to navigate the intricate process of settling the overwhelming debts as much as possible.

Despite his heartfelt efforts and the completion of his own barrister studies, the burden of the financial aftermath and the inability to sustain his education in London weighed heavily on Rajini's shoulders. The financial constraints left him with no choice but to make the difficult decision to bid farewell to his aspirations in London.

With a heavy heart and a resolved spirit, Rajini made the poignant decision to return to his homeland, India. This event marking a turning point in his life's journey as he embarked on the path that destiny had set forth for him to fulfill the dream of continuing his revolution and Hartman's aspiration of Rajini becoming a great leader.

Rajini remained deeply grateful to Frederick Hartman for the chance he had been given. He viewed his education not as a personal achievement

but as a powerful tool for empowering his people and advancing the cause of justice and equality.

His revolutionary spirit had been fortified with knowledge, insight and purpose. The day arrived for him to return home to India, to his wife and now eight-year-old daughter. Towards his fellow countrymen living under the boots of British colonialism and Indian authoritarianism, he bore new lessons of dissent. Lessons that would set alight the sparking embers of an impending rebellion.

Chapter 10
Homeward Bound: Rajini's Journey on the Montgomery

Every journey carries a story within it, a tale of anticipation, reflection, and the connection between distant lands.

At a bustling English port: Rajini Reddy standing by the Montgomery, a ship docked at the port. Having completed his studies in England, stood at the threshold of a new chapter in his life.

With a heart full of memories and a mind brimming with newfound knowledge, he stepped onto the Montgomery – a vessel that would carry him back to his homeland. The ship was a microcosm of its own, a diverse collection of people from different corners of the world, all bound by the shared experience of travel. As the ship sailed, Rajini often found himself on the deck, gazing at the vast expanse of the sea, lost in thought.

He struck up conversations with fellow passengers, sharing stories of their respective journeys and cultures. Rajini's insatiable thirst for knowledge was not confined to textbooks – he sought to learn from every individual he met.

In the solitude of his cabin, he poured over his notes, reflecting on the lessons he had learned and the ideas he intended to share back home.

A Crimson tide

Amidst the tumult of the crimson tide,

Where fervent hearts in unity collide,

Humanity's flame, a vision strong and bright,

Awakens dreams of justice, endless light.

Oh, comrade's spirit, fierce and unconfined,

In futuristic dreams, a crimson fire enshrined,

A world where wealth and power are shared alike,

Where chains of class, inequality we strike.

Yet caution whispers, tread with wary gaze,

For tyrants often cloak in righteous haze,

In seeking equity, let freedom thrive,

Lest noble aims to tyranny connive.

Oh, the soul's echoes through the ages ring,

In pursuit of justice, let true freedom sing,

Humanity's dream, a noble quest to bear,

With open hearts, a just world we declare.

------ Rajini

The journey was not without its challenges. The ship encountered storms that tested the resolve of the passengers and crew. As the ship battled the forces of nature, Rajini found parallels between the voyage and the struggles of his people. He listened to the stories of the crew, who spoke of their own hardships and dreams, realizing that despite different backgrounds, they shared a common humanity. As the ship neared the shores of India, Rajini's heart quickened with a mix of emotions – anticipation, nostalgia, and a burning desire to contribute to his homeland.

The ship's crew worked in harmony, coordinating their efforts to ensure a safe and smooth arrival. In a farewell speech to his fellow passengers, Rajini spoke of the journey as a metaphor for the shared aspirations of humanity.

And so, the Montgomery, which had carried Rajini across the seas, brought him back to the land that held his heart.

As Rajini stepped onto Indian soil, he carried with him the experiences, knowledge, and determination he had gained during his journey.

Rajini facing the horizon, a smile of determination on his face. His journey on the Montgomery was more than a physical voyage – it was a passage of self-discovery, a connection between distant lands, and a bridge between cultures.

His return would mark the beginning of a new phase in his life, one where he would channel his experiences and education into the pursuit of justice and a better future for his people.

The ship's horn sounded as it pulled into Madras port. Rajini took a deep breath, embracing the familiar scent of his homeland after years abroad. Parvathi held little Lakshmi's hand tightly, filled with equal parts joy and apprehension.

How much has changed in my absence? Rajini wondered.

Stepping onto the crowded docks, Rajini was greeted by a trusted friend. "Welcome back, brother," said Ravi, a longtime supporter of Rajini's crusade against injustice. "The people have awaited your return eagerly. But the oppressors grow more ruthless by the day." Rajini nodded gravely. "Then we have no time to delay. Please, gather our people. I wish to speak to them tonight."

Chapter 11
A Changed Vision

That evening, dozens crammed into Ravi's small home to hear Rajini speak. He told them of his experiences in England, the books he had read, and the ideologies he now embraced. "The individual struggles of our villages are but a microcosm of a global struggle between imperial oppressors and the working class," Rajini declared. "Our liberation lies in unity and revolution."

"Our liberation lies in unity and revolution."

He spoke passionately against imperialism, authoritarianism and the tyranny of the caste and class system. He articulated a vision for an egalitarian society - a socialist India where farmers owned the land they tilled, workers controlled the fruits of their labor, and all people regardless of caste, creed or religion lived as equals. His audience listened raptly, never having heard such radical notions before.

"Educate yourselves," Rajini urged them.

"Learn your rights. Organize yourselves.

Only through knowledge and solidarity can we break free of our bondage."

Many approached him afterwards, pledging their support to the burgeoning resistance movement.

Soon Rajini, along with Ravi and other followers, began mobilizing oppressed communities throughout the region. They organized rallies and inspired workers to form unions, distributed pamphlets on socialism, and led civil disobedience campaigns against unjust British taxes.

A wave of electricity coursed through the people - **here at last we have a leader willing to speak truth to power**.

Rajini and parvathi talk about his life in England and her life here in his absence.

A quiet evening in Rajini and Parvathi's home. They sit together on the porch, a gentle breeze rustling the leaves.

Rajini, Gazing into the distance, says; "Parvathi, it's hard to believe how far we've come, isn't it?"

Parvathi Nods, Indeed, Rajini. From the days of our childhood, when we played by the river, to now, sitting here, married and sharing our dreams.

He smiles and says, yes, and one of the most remarkable experiences in my life was studying in England. It's so different from our village.

Tell me more, Rajini. What was it like?

Rajini Pauses, (reflecting), Well, Parvathi, England is a place of contrasts. The cities are bustling with activity, like our village fair, but on a grander scale. People from all corners of the world come together.

Parvathi: [Wide-eyed] That must have been exciting.

Rajini: [Nods] It was, but it was also a reminder of the vast disparities in the world. I saw towering skyscrapers and luxurious cars, but I also witnessed poverty and inequality.

Parvathi: [Thoughtful] Did it change you, Rajini? Your perspective on life?

Rajini: [Sighs] It did, Parvathi. It made me realize that the world is a complex place. There's so much to learn, so many ideas to explore. I understood the power of education and how it can bring about change.

Parvathi: [Touches Rajini's hand] You've always had a thirst for knowledge, Rajini. It's one of the things I admire most about you.

Rajini: [Smiles warmly] And that's why I'm so excited to share what I've learned with our people. To bring the ideas of justice, equality, and unity to our village.

Parvathi: [Grateful] I believe in you, Rajini. Your experiences in England will make our journey toward a better life even more meaningful.

Rajini: [Squeezes Parvathi's hand] Together, Parvathi, we'll create a brighter future for our community. One where every individual is valued, just as I value you. Tell me now, how was it here in my absence? It must have been difficult to you here. How foolish was I to leave you alone here!

Parvathi: [Sighs] Rajini, I've often thought about those days when you were away in England. It was a challenging time for me here.

Rajini: [Concerned] I can only imagine, Parvathi. I'm sorry for leaving you behind during those difficult years.

Parvathi: [Touches Rajini's hand] Don't blame yourself, Rajini. You had your dreams to pursue, and I knew that. Besides, I had my own battles to fight here.

Rajini: [Curious] What do you mean, Parvathi? What happened while I was away?

Parvathi: [Pauses, her expression somber] Well, Rajini, you know how the feudal lords in our village can be. Without you here, they saw an opportunity to assert their dominance.

Rajini: [Frowning] They didn't harm you, did they?

Parvathi: [Shakes her head] No, not physically. But they tried to intimidate me, to pressure me into submission. They wanted me to convince you to abandon your ideas of justice and equality.

Rajini: Those feudal wolves! How dare they!

Parvathi: [Placing her hand on Rajini's shoulder] I knew you'd be upset, Rajini, but I didn't give in to their threats. I remembered your words and your dreams. I knew I had to be strong for both of us.

Rajini: Parvathi, you've always been my strength. I couldn't have asked for a more courageous and resilient partner.

Parvathi: [Smiles] We've faced our share of challenges, Rajini, and we'll face more in the future. But as long as we stand together, we can overcome anything.

Rajini: [Nods] You're right, Parvathi. Our love and our shared vision for a better society will guide us through whatever comes our way.

They sit in companionable silence, the lanterns flickering in the night.

Parvathi: [Softly] I'm so proud of you, Rajini. You've returned from England with knowledge and ideas that can change our village, our lives, and the lives of so many others.

Rajini: [Touched] And I'm proud of you, Parvathi. You held our community together when I was away, and you never wavered in your belief in justice and equality.

They share a loving glance, their bond stronger than ever.

Few days later…..

A discussion with villagers regarding the social revolution

A peaceful evening in the village, where Rajini gathers the villagers for a thought-provoking discussion about society and its transformation. As the sun dipped below the horizon, painting the sky in hues of orange and pink, Rajini invited the villagers to assemble in the heart of their village. Rajini, standing before the villagers, his demeanor calm yet filled with purpose. The villagers, young and old, had gathered to engage in a conversation that transcended the boundaries of their everyday lives. Rajini started explaining the principles of justice and equality and also about the societies and their transformation.

The discussion began with Rajini painting a vivid picture of the challenges and lifestyles of early humans. Rajini in his voice resonating with conviction, "My fellow comrades, tonight we gather not just to talk about change but to embark on a journey towards a more just and equitable society." Let us journey through time and contemplate the remarkable transformation of humanity. From hunter-gatherers to social beings, our story is one of evolution and interconnectedness. In the earliest days of our species, we were nomadic hunter-gatherers, relying on our primal instincts for survival. As the time passed, we realized that we were stronger together. Communities formed, and we discovered the power of cooperation. With the advent of agriculture, we moved from nomadic life to settled societies. This marked a pivotal moment in our history. Our transformation from hunter-gatherers to social beings gave birth to culture, art, and the intricate web of social bonds that define us today.

The discussion expanded to including the challenges and benefits of transitioning to an agrarian society. Rajini's voice resonated with passion as he continued to guide the villagers through this profound narrative. The villagers contemplated the beauty and complexity of the human experience, a tapestry woven through millennia of evolution. The villagers, their faces reflecting a mix of determination and curiosity, nodded in agreement, engaging in this transformative dialogue.

"My dear friends, let us commence a voyage through time to explore the astounding evolution of the human mind – a journey that has shaped the very essence of who we are. In the earliest days of humanity, our ancestors relied on instinct and intuition for survival. Their minds were honed by the challenges of the natural world.

With the development of language, our ancestors took a monumental leap. Language became the bridge that connected minds, enabling cooperation and shared knowledge.

Abstract thinking marked a turning point. It allowed us to conceptualize ideas, envision the future, and lay the foundations of civilization.

Empathy and compassion emerged as pillars of our humanity, fostering cooperation, and the intricate web of social bonds that define our existence."

"A social revolution is not about overthrowing one system for another; it's about dismantling the very foundations of oppression and inequality.

Our revolution is not just about changing the external world; it's about empowering each and every one of us to be architects of our own destinies. Our revolution begins with education, with knowledge. It begins by challenging the norms that have held us back for too long.

My friends, we stand at a crossroads in history. We have the power to shape the destiny of our society, to transform it into something better.

Society is not a fixed entity; it is a living organism that can evolve. And it is our collective responsibility to ensure that it evolves for the better.

Empathy is the foundation of societal transformation. We must understand each other's pain to build a society based on justice and equality.

Unity is our greatest strength. When we come together with a shared vision, there is no challenge too great."

Rajini's words were a beacon of hope, a reminder that change was not only possible but essential as the wisdom of the ages was passed down from one generation to the next, igniting a spark of enlightenment.

The villagers nodded in agreement, their hearts open to the idea of change, their faces reflecting a mixture of curiosity and determination.

The discussion unfolded, with villagers sharing their personal stories of hardship, discrimination, discussing plans, outlining steps for the revolution and dreams of a better future.

The villagers began sharing their personal stories, their struggles, and the challenges they faced in their daily lives. The villagers spoke freely, their voices gaining strength as they realized the power of collective action and unity.

The villagers engaged in thoughtful conversations, exploring the nuances of their society and envisioning a path towards transformation. The discussion evolved into ideas for collective action, strategies to raise awareness, and plans to challenge the injustices they faced. As the night wore on, plans began to take shape.

They discussed strategies for raising awareness, organizing peaceful protests, and building a movement. In the stillness of the night, surrounded by the collective will for change, Rajini, Parvathi, and the villagers laid the foundation for a social revolution that would shape the destiny of their village. Rajini and Parvathi listened intently; their hearts filled with hope that this dialogue would ignite the spark of change.

As the sun dipped below the horizon, the villagers and Rajini shared a newfound appreciation for the journey of humanity, from the primal instincts of survival to the intricate tapestry of social interconnectedness.

Chapter 12
The Awakening

The birth of Rajini's son Ramu in 1912, brought a brief respite from his frenetic schedule organizing the movement. Parvathi smiled, watching her husband gently cradle the newborn. "What future do you envision for our children?" she asked.

Rajini kissed Ramu's tiny forehead. "They will grow up in a free India, as equals to all children, unshackled by caste or creed. I wish for Lakshmi to become a teacher, empowering other girls with education. For Ramu, a life of dignity, liberty, and justice." Parvathi nodded tearfully, sharing his dreams, tears rolling down.

But Rajini knew this future is hung in a delicate balance. Powerful forces worked to undermine the movement's growth. British authorities had begun a campaign of targeted arrests, raids and propaganda to stamp out early revolutionary activity. But most alarming were the renewed attacks by Somi's henchmen with the support of British.

The land owning Zamindars had grown increasingly hostile as Rajini's message of empowerment among lower castes, workers and peasants began threatening their hegemony. One night, armed thugs brutally attacked a workers' union meeting organized by Rajini. Though he helped the injured escape, three farm laborers were killed in the skirmish.

"This was Somi attempting to silence us through terror," Rajini told Parvathi later, his jaw set in quiet fury. "But we will only grow louder."

Parvathi wrung her hands anxiously. "Must you antagonize the lords and the British so directly?

Think of the children..."

Rajini grasped her shoulders firmly. "**That is all I think about**. If we do not act now, Lakshmi and Ramu's generation will continue languishing in the same servitude that has oppressed us for decades. We must save the future of India's youth, though the path be strewn with obstacles."

Parvathi saw the blazing conviction in her husband's eyes. She realized his ambitions extended far beyond their family's security - he worked tirelessly for the freedom and rights of all people in this land. Though fearful for his safety, Parvathi vowed to support Rajini in this selfless crusade.

In the following months, Rajini spearheaded a civil disobedience movement against British salt taxes that galvanized thousands across southern India. He organized protests to spread socialist thought among students.

He gave rousing speeches promoting sweat equity farming collectives and worker-owned cooperatives, detailing his vision for an egalitarian society.

From dusty rural villages to crowded city streets, Rajini became a household name. Some decried him a dangerous radical undermining societal values and British rule. But many more saw a dedicated leader willing to sacrifice everything to help the marginalized dream of a life liberated from suffering and servitude.

A brave voice beckoning oppressed people towards a new dawn.

Word of Rajini's defiant activism had spread like wildfire across southern India. In remote villages, city slums and factory floors - marginalized people whispered his name, this fearless crusader challenging oppressive traditions and colonial rule. To many, Rajini represented a new path to dignity and justice.

Under the cover of darkness, when the world had settled into a serene hush, Rajini and Parvathi embarked on a clandestine mission. The quiet village nights, where the soft glow of lanterns illuminates a small gathering of villagers.

Rajini and Parvathi stand before them, their dedication shining through, starts teaching the adult villagers to read and write. The adults, many of whom had never held a book before, gathered around, their eagerness to learn palpable, their faces a mix of anticipation and hope.

The teaching was not just about letters and words; it was a transformation of hearts and minds, a journey towards empowerment.

Rajini's words on the importance of education "Education is the key to breaking the chains of oppression. With knowledge, we can rise above our circumstances." Armed with the flickering light of lanterns and the power of knowledge, they had made it their mission to teach the adults of the village how to read and write, by patiently teaching the villagers, their voices gentle and encouraging. The villagers practicing their newly acquired reading and writing skills

Night after night, the nearby villages saw a quiet revolution as adults who had once been denied the chance to learn began to unlock the doors to their own potential. For Rajini and Parvathi, this late-night endeavor was a testament to their unwavering commitment to justice and equality.

Parvathi's passionate words on the power of education resounded in many of the nearby villages and irritated many oppressors.

"When we educate ourselves, we empower ourselves. We become the architects of our destiny."

The village nights, once filled with darkness, were now illuminated by the beacon of knowledge, dispelling the shadows of ignorance.

Rajini and Parvathi with chalkboards, books, and a group of eager villagers in the quiet village nights has become a common picture over the months and in many villages.

The lanterns cast a soft, warm glow on Rajini and Parvathi as they stood before the villagers, ready to impart a deeper understanding of the world through education.

Rajini and Parvathi's nightly teachings were not just about reading and writing; they were a declaration of hope, a promise of a brighter future for many villages where the seeds of education had been sown and were beginning to flourish.

They delved into a range of subjects. Their teaching went beyond just basic literacy. It was a comprehensive education that aimed to empower the villagers in various aspects of life. They discussed history, helping the villagers understand the context of their struggles and the importance of learning from the past.

Rajini in an Inspiring tone: "Education isn't just about reading and writing. It's about understanding the world around us. It's about critical thinking, problem-solving, and empowerment."

Rajini explaining historical events; "History is our teacher. By knowing the past, we can shape a better future."

On those fruitful nights, many of the villagers took their first steps in learning mathematics. Their faces illuminated by the lantern light.

Parvathi encouraging the villagers demonstrating mathematical concepts "Mathematics isn't just numbers; it's a language of logic. It can help us plan for a better tomorrow.

Mathematics will become a tool for practical problem-solving, from overcoming exploitation to managing resources and making informed decisions."

Rajini and Parvathi reading stories aloud.

Literature is a window to the human experience. It helps us understand our own feelings and the feelings of others. Literature and storytelling allowed the villagers to explore different perspectives and emotions, fostering empathy and creativity. The Villagers exploring literature, their faces reflecting the emotions of the stories.

Parvathi explaining scientific principles;

"Science is the language of nature. It helps us make sense of the world and empowers us to find solutions."

Introduction to Science opened their minds to the wonders of the natural world, encouraging curiosity and a thirst for knowledge enlightening their minds and started the process of eradicating blind beliefs. Some of the interested villagers engaged in discussions, pondering over complex topics.

Rajini addressing issues of inequality:

Discussions on social issues were at the core of their teachings, encouraging villagers to question societal norms and envision a more just society. Villagers got the taste of learning about social issues, discussing equality and justice.

Passionately "We must confront injustice and work together for a fairer world. Education gives us the tools to do just that."

Each night, Rajini and Parvathi guided their students through a comprehensive education that was not just about knowledge but also about enlightenment, empowerment, and transformation.

Rajini, Parvathi, and the villagers, their lantern-lit faces filled with determination, the village lit with the flames of education burned bright, lighting the way to a better future.

Chapter 13
A Journey beyond Social Boundaries

"Thanga Muthu", the Tamil feudal lord and his henchmen looked on uneasily as hundreds gathered at one of Rajini's rallies on the outskirts of Madras city. Men and women, young and old - all drawn by his fiery oratory and vision of liberation.

"Too long have we suffered the indignities of imperial subjugation, class and caste tyranny," Rajini thundered. "But the light of self-rule, equality and prosperity shall soon dawn upon India! That is, if her people unite and seize this destiny for themselves!"

Loud cheers erupted from the electrified crowd. These rural laborers and city workers had found a voice for their struggles in Rajini's rousing message.

"Organize yourselves and claim your rights, my friends. The oppressors thrive only because we remain divided. But together, as one unbreakable force, we hold the power to shake the foundations of injustice!"

These directly defiant words made the lord's henchmen squirm with discomfort. They knew that losing their grip over the lower classes meant losing everything. So they hastily dispersed the energized rally before Rajini's speech could mobilize the masses into open rebellion.

But the brute strength of the lords and the British could not extinguish the hopes and dreams already ignited in people's hearts.

The kindling of change had been lit, soon to spread as an unstoppable wildfire across all of India.

In the following months, Rajini led other civil disobedience initiatives, strikes and grassroots campaigns alongside workers, challenging inhumane labor conditions. He organized night schools to educate the children of untouchables, defying caste prohibitions. He gave legal aid to abused women and lower castes, empowering them to fight back against generations of exploitation.

"Why do you rile them up and make impossible promises?" Parvathi asked worriedly as Rajini returned home one night. "You know very well the oppressors will not relinquish their power so easily."

Rajini smiled and embraced his wife.

"I do not make false promises. I only awaken what already lies dormant in their hearts - the irresistible desire for freedom and dignity. Once stirred, that longing cannot be suppressed.

Ours will be a long and perilous struggle. But I have faith we shall overcome."

Parvathi sighed, knowing she could not dissuade her husband once his mind was set. She could only stand by him on this thorny path.

That night, after the children were asleep, Rajini and Parvathi lay gazing up at the stars. She noticed a peculiar glint in his eyes.

"You seem different since returning from that salt march protest," Parvathi remarked. "I sense a change in your spirit."

Rajini turned to her. "It was incredible to witness thousands transcend their fears that day. Temple priests, people branded as untouchables, Muslims - all walking alongside each other as equals, united by a higher calling. I saw then that this dream could truly be reality. "He clasped Parvathi's hand tightly. "Those people were meek and afraid when they arrived. But after marching together, shoulders back and heads held high, they realized the indomitable power they possessed as one."

Rajini's voice quavered with emotion. "Our efforts are awakening people from placid resignation to their fate. We are lighting a fire in their souls that no tyranny can extinguish. That is a flame bright with hope." Parvathi was moved by the raw conviction in his words. She prayed this blaze of change would remain a glowing ember of progress, not turn into a destructive forest fire bringing only ruin.

"Do you remember the village fair incident?" asked Parvathi.

How could I forget that! Smiled Rajini. "Do you remember how we got married?" asked Parvathi. Rajini remembered those days.

Love, they say, knows no boundaries. And for Rajini Reddy, love would lead him on a journey that challenged societal norms and ignited the flames of change. Rajini and Parvathi's childhood interactions.

As children, Rajini and Parvathi shared innocent moments, their friendship blossoming into a bond that transcended caste lines. Rajini and Parvathi playing near a river

But as they grew older, the realities of the world cast a shadow on their love, for Rajini hailed from an upper caste while Parvathi was from a lower caste. Rajini and Parvathi kept stealing glances, but less talking. Despite the societal pressures and expectations, their feelings for each other only grew stronger, a testament to the depth of their connection.

A lively village fair

Sometimes, heroism isn't defined by grand battles, but by the small moments when one person stands up for what's right. In the heart of the vibrant village fair, a simple act of courage would forever etch Rajini Reddy's name into the annals of history. Parvathi, Rajini's beloved, found herself targeted by a group of harassers who sought to tarnish the spirit of the festive occasion.

Parvathi was being harassed by a group of rowdy men.

Parvathi's in distress, and the harassers laughing

Their taunts and harassment were like thorns, threatening to pierce the joy that surrounded the fair.

Rajini's determined expression: But Rajini Reddy, a man of courage and conviction, could not stand idle by. With a heart afire with righteousness, Rajini stepped forward to defend Parvathi's honor and dignity.

In the midst of a crowd, he faced the teasers, his voice carrying the weight of his determination to protect the one he loved. His words were like a rallying cry, challenging the teasers' actions and demanding respect for every individual, regardless of gender.

As the harassers faltered under Rajini's unwavering gaze, the crowd around them shifted from spectators to allies in a quiet stand against injustice. In that moment, Rajini's actions spoke volumes about his character, his courage, and his commitment to love and dignity. The harassers, their arrogance shattered, retreated in the face of the collective will of the people.

Rajini's interaction with Parvathi, their eyes sharing a moment of connection. As the crowd applauded Rajini's courage, his eyes found Parvathi's, and in that shared glance, they knew that their love was stronger than any adversity, their hands clasped. And so, in that seemingly ordinary moment at the village fair, Rajini Reddy became a hero, not through violence, but through the power of his conviction to stand up for justice, love, and the dignity of every individual.

Rajini and Parvathi shared a quiet moment. Rajini knew that if they were to be together, they would need to overcome the deeply ingrained biases of their society. Seeking guidance from a wise elder, Rajini learned of the struggles and sacrifices made by those who had dared to challenge the status quo.

With newfound determination, Rajini not only won just Parvathi's heart, but also the acceptance of her family. Rajini started helping with chores, participating in local festivities. He engaged with Parvathi's family, proving his sincerity and commitment through actions that spoke louder than words.

A tense meeting happened between Rajini and Parvathi's family. In a pivotal moment, Rajini faced Parvathi's family, their expressions a mix of skepticism and uncertainty.

Rajini was passionately expressing his love for Parvathi. With unwavering conviction, Rajini expressed his love for Parvathi, vowing to stand by her side no matter the challenges they would face.

Parvathi's eyes were filled with hope. Parvathi's hope and trust in Rajini's words would be the driving force that emboldened him to confront societal prejudices. Faced with opposition, Rajini and Parvathi made the courageous decision, to defy the norms that sought to keep them apart.

Rajini and Parvathi took their vows, pledging their love and commitment to each other. Rajini and Parvathi's life together, has not only their joys but their challenges. Their journey was not without challenges, but their love was an unwavering beacon of hope, an inspiration to those who believed in breaking down barriers. And so, in their love story, Rajini and Parvathi demonstrated the power of love to transcend boundaries, to challenge norms, and to pave the way for a future where love knows no caste, no prejudice, and no limits.

The coming months were a whirlwind of organizing and action. From the tea estates of Assam to the salt flats of Gujarat, Rajini spearheaded nonviolent civil disobedience that challenged British economic exploitation. He gave impassioned speeches promoting worker's rights, women's equality and Lower caste empowerment.

At times even Rajini was astounded by the response. Thousands flocked to his rallies, hungry for his galvanizing message. Oppressed peoples once resigned to their fate were now infused with revolutionary zeal.

A powerful movement was stirring, and Rajini stood at its heart as both orchestrator and lightning rod.

But the forces loath to lose their unchecked power were closely watching too. The land owning feudals grew anxious as their laborers became more organized and defiant.

The British colonial administration seethed as Rajini's actions threatened their unrestrained resource extraction and authority.

"This rabble-rouser is radicalizing the uneducated masses. Left unchecked, he will upend civilized society!" Somi fumed to the British commissioner one sweltering afternoon. "We must arrest these treasonous activities immediately."

The stern commissioner stroked his moustache pensively. "Agreed this growing unrest must be firmly curtailed. But arresting their leader could elevate him into a martyr. We must discredit Rajini as a violent agitator in the people's eyes first."

Somi nodded slowly as an insidious plan took shape in his mind. "I believe you are right, Sir. My men will handle this menace soon enough..."

Under the surface, powerful forces were aligning to resist Rajini's crusade for freedom and justice. But he remained undeterred, drawing strength from the groundswell of momentum and support from the newly awakened masses.

Chapter 14
The Resistance

Rajini stepped off the podium to thunderous applause, his voice hoarse after delivering an impassioned two-hour speech on economic justice.

As the exhilarated crowd dispersed, Rajini felt a tug on his kurta.

He looked down to see a disheveled old woman with teary eyes. My son finally stood up to our cruel landlord and refused to work without fair pay, she said. But now he has been beaten and thrown in jail.

"Please help us, great one!"

Rajini clasped her hands reassuringly.

Do not worry, Amma. I will personally see that your son is freed and treated justly. This is why we must keep fighting. Such encounters were growing more frequent as Rajini's fiery words stirred the oppressed to take action. But those determined to maintain the status quo would not give up their power easily.

The following week, Rajini was scheduled to speak at a worker's union rally in the industrial city hub of Coimbatore. But as he approached the venue, he was alarmed to see plumes of smoke rising ahead. A mob sent by angry factory owners had attacked the workers before they could gather, with the police simply watching idle. Rajini helped the bloodied workers escape to safety, but the violent suppression of their voices enraged him.

That night at home, Lakshmi could see her father's hands trembling with fury as he recounted the incident to her mother. Those cowardly vultures, attacking unarmed people! Rajini spat. But this will only strengthen the workers' resolve.

Lakshmi had rarely seen her usually tranquil father so shaken with anger. She worried where this intensifying conflict might lead, but kept silent.

Parvathi tried calming Rajini, urging him to focus instead on his university lecture tour promoting social empowerment. You are wasting time on these impoverished masses who cannot fathom your ideals, she said. It is the educated elite you must convince to drive real progress.

Rajini shook his head adamantly. No. The privileged will only support superficial change that serves their interests.

My faith rests with the workers, farmers and all oppressed people. They must lead the struggle for their own liberation.

Lakshmi smiled proudly at her father's unwavering principles, but Parvathi wrung her hands anxiously. She feared Rajini was raising dangerous forces beyond his control.

Nonetheless, Rajini continued energizing crowds across the region with talks on overthrowing imperialism, feudalism and caste hegemony through mass mobilization. He rattled the status quo with worker strikes, rallies and nonviolent resistance. A defiant wave was swelling, with Rajini at its crest.

But others remained fiercely resistant to this brewing revolution. At a lavish party of landowners and British elites, Rajini's name elicited scowls and muttered threats. He is a cancer infecting the uneducated with dangerous foreign ideologies, a feudal lord growled. We must excise this tumor before it spreads!

But a wily old British officer raised a hand. Brute force only increases his allure as a radical hero. We must instead erode this scoundrel's influence from within. Turn his followers against him. Remind the masses that he is simply chasing a petty personal vengeance, not their interests.

The land owners nodded slowly, cognizant of the public's growing reverence for Rajini. Yes, a cunning plan was needed to protect their generations old power and wealth. So, anti-Rajini propaganda began circulating, calling him a violent fraud misleading the ignorant. British authorities claimed that his ideology bred only chaos and disorder. Meanwhile, work dried up mysteriously for those affiliated with Rajini's unions, forcing hungry families to distance themselves from his movement.

But Rajini remained unperturbed amidst this rising resistance.

Chapter 15
Heart Wrenching

Not even betrayal and abandonment by some followers could extinguish his revolutionary spirit. Because he knew a formidable tide was stirring, one that could no longer be suppressed by the old order. The people had awoken, and there was no lulling them back to sleep.

Standing at a vantage point and waving at familiar faces passing by.

Rajini had cleared his schedule today, ignoring even urgent movement matters. For now, his universe revolved around this tiny girl whom he loved infinitely.

As they walked hand in hand back home later that night, Lakshmi paused to admire the full moon's silvery reflection on a pond nearby. Rajini sat on the grassy bank, lost in the innocent joy radiating from his daughter's face. A refreshing breeze stirred, untroubled by the burdens weighing heavy on Rajini's shoulders.

Suddenly, the serene night was shattered by a blood curdling scream. Rajini leapt up to see bullock carts barreling towards them, filled with vicious-looking men wielding torches and knives. Before he could react, the thugs had surrounded them. Rajini sheltered Lakshmi protectively beneath him, ready to lay down his life for hers.

The brutish men hurled abuses, accusing Rajini of poisoning local peoples' minds and undermining civilized society. How dare you fill these simpletons with treasonous ideas, warping them against age-old traditions and the British Raj that maintains order here! their leader spat. Rajini glared back defiantly. It is you who poison society through oppression and injustice! My people thirst only for human dignity and self-rule.

Your reign of tyranny is at its end!

The angry men moved closer, weapons glinting. Then let us rid the world of this toxin infecting our youth, starting with your own tainted spawn!

Before Rajini could react, they tore Lakshmi from his arms. The screams that left his throat became primal, inhuman roars. With superhuman strength he flung himself at the barbarians, fighting desperately to reach his daughter.

His training in Kalari helped to knock down about forty men, but the savage men greatly outnumbered him. Their knives plunged in unison, piercing the helpless child's small body again and again.

Rajini let loose the beast inside him and started chopping whoever came in the way. By the time he reached his child, all the perpetuators who came to attack lied lifeless with mutilated body parts and blood everywhere.

As he reached his child's body, an agonized wail vent out, his spirit shattered into a million jagged shards. He crumpled to the ground, the heinous act that unfolded before his eyes burning forever into his consciousness.

Rajini cradled his daughter's body, rocking back and forth dementedly. Tears flowed until nothing remained inside him - only a cold, black abyss where his soul had been.

It was well past midnight when Rajini staggered back home, haunted eyes staring straight ahead. His companions rushed to help their blood drenched comrade, but he shoved past them towards the bedroom. Parvathi awoke to a nightmare - her husband drenched in their daughter's blood, clutching her body.

A guttural cry escaped her very being. For hours, the grieving couple sat huddled together, inconsolable.

Rajini finally spoke in a dead voice: It was Somi Reddy's henchmen. His icy gaze turned to steel. The feudal oppressors have always attacked me indirectly, through those I love most.

First my parents, now my blameless innocent Lakshmi.

It ends today. This time I will answer them directly.

Parvathi trembled uncontrollably, begging Rajini not to allow this abominable act to push him into violence. But the light in his eyes told her the man she loved was gone. In his place sat a figure hardened by loss and consumed by cold vengeance.

At dawn, Rajini kissed Lakshmi's forehead tenderly one final time. Then he stormed out to the courtyard where hundreds had gathered, hearing the tragic news. An eerie hush fell over the crowd as their incensed leader emerged.

For too long we have suffered brutality meted out against our loved ones, Rajini thundered. But remember this - the oppressor only triumphs when violence goes unanswered! Atrocities unpunished multiply.

But resistance confronted halts evil in its tracks!

Chapter 16
Somi – The oppressor

Vengeance will not bring our Lakshmi back, Parvathi pleaded, clutching his arm. Rajini slowly turned his vacant eyes upon her. You are right, my love. Nothing can restore our loss. But I can now unfold the purpose of my life.

To ensure no other endures the pain we have.

With that, he strode away. Parvathi collapsed in anguish, her beloved husband transformed utterly from humanitarian crusader to vessel of vengeance.

But in the crowd's eyes blazed fury stirred by Rajini's call to resist. His tragedy had become their rallying cry against injustice. And it would soon ignite a wildfire.

Somi Reddy reclined leisurely on the verandah of his palatial estate, enjoying the mild winter morning. He took a long drag from his imported cigar, watching laborers sweating in the distant fields that generated his vast wealth.

All was well in his world. Or so he thought, until an anxious servant came rushing out. Dora! Dora!, a massive mob is approaching! They look ready to burn the estate down!

Somi Reddy lurched up furiously. What nonsense is this? Drive those vermin away at once! But the servant shook his head. There are hundreds of them, dora. Led by Rajini Reddy himself! We cannot stop them...

Somi Reddy paled. Ever since the brutal murder of Rajini's daughter, he had feared this moment of reckoning. Quickly he assembled his henchmen. Fortify the manor immediately! That rabid dog will not touch me as long as I draw breath! Soon the estate was swarming with hundreds of Rajini's livid followers.

Somi Reddy watched apprehensively from a window upstairs as the crusader himself approached. Gone was the defiant idealism that once marked Rajini's face. In its place Somi Reddy saw only icy, ruthless purpose.

Rajini raised a trembling finger towards his nemesis. For too long you have escaped justice while destroying countless innocents. But your depravity ends today! With that, the inflamed mob charged forward, bellowing vengefully. They tore down manor gates, smashed windows, and ransacked rooms searching for the elusive Reddy.

Henchmen who resisted were viciously beaten down. Upstairs, Somi Reddy trembled behind locked doors as the mayhem unfolded. How quickly the peasants forget my generosity, he thought bitterly. All the loans given, jobs provided over generations overturned in a moment of madness by that rabble rouser!

The bedroom door suddenly splintered open under repeated blows. Rajini burst in, with a sickle in the right hand and a hammer in his left hand, eyes aflame with long-simmering rage.

The Moment of reckoning was finally here. He roughly grabbed the cowering oppressor. Did you think your lofty position would forever shield you from the people's justice? The oppressed have now opened their eyes. Your poisonous reign over them has ended!

Dragging the whimpering landlord down, Rajini presented him triumphantly before the frenzied horde. After today, never again will this parasite profit from the common man's sweat and blood! Their roar was thunderous, hungry for vengeance.

Parvathi pushed desperately through the crowd. She fell at her husband's feet, pleading for mercy and non-violence. This is not our way! If we also stoop to barbarism, how can we claim moral superiority?

Rajini's face softened ever so slightly as he gazed upon his beloved wife. A glimmer of his old self stirred within. But then his eyes hardened again as he turned to address the impassioned gathering. She speaks wisdom. Retribution cannot become our purpose, lest we become the evil we fight. The people's court will decide this vermin's fate.

Somi Reddy shall get the justice he denied my Lakshmi!

The oppressor still showing his venomous fangs by a two tongued argument, but could he beat the intellectual mind of Rajini in the argument.

The climax of the confrontation came when Rajini Reddy, with a fiery determination burning in his eyes, challenged Somi Reddy to face the consequences of his actions.

It was a moment of reckoning—a symbolic clash between the forces of justice and oppression. The outcome of their final confrontation would not only determine the fate of these two individuals but also resonate with the destiny of an entire region.

The battle of words and ideals raged on, leaving the outcome uncertain. The mansion of Somi Reddy, once a symbol of his power, now stood witness to a pivotal moment in history—a moment that would ultimately define the legacy of both Rajini Reddy and the struggle against oppressive forces.

Rajini (R): Somi Reddy, your fascist ideology is a poison that divides society based on race, nationality, and class. It promotes a hierarchical system where a select few hold power and manipulate the masses to maintain their control. Socialism, on the other hand, aims to eradicate these divisions by establishing a classless society where the working class collectively holds power and resources are shared equitably.

Somi Reddy (SR): Rajini, your socialist ideals might sound appealing, but they are unrealistic and dangerous. Socialism has led to economic inefficiency and stagnation wherever it's been tried. A strong nation requires a strong leader who can make swift decisions without being bogged down by the bureaucracy inherent in your socialist system.

R: Strong leaders often lead to authoritarianism and tyranny. Your fascist ideology ignores the value of individual rights and freedoms. Socialism seeks to empower individuals by removing the chains of exploitation and ensuring that everyone has access to education, healthcare, and a dignified life.

SR: Individual rights mean nothing in a society that's torn apart by internal strife and external threats. Our nation needs unity and discipline to thrive. Fascism recognizes the importance of national identity and cultural heritage, ensuring that our people share a common purpose and stand together against any challenges.

R: Your emphasis on national identity often masks exclusion and discrimination. Fascist regimes have a history of suppressing dissent and oppressing underprivileged groups. Socialism strives for a world where diversity is celebrated and all individuals are treated with dignity, regardless of their background.

SR: Socialism's idealistic vision ignores the complexities of human nature. People have different talents and motivations. A meritocratic society, as advocated by fascism, rewards hard work and innovation. It doesn't burden the productive with the weight of supporting those who contribute less.

R: Meritocracy in fascism often becomes a guise for preserving the privileges of the elite. Socialism ensures that everyone's basic needs are met, allowing individuals to pursue their passions and contribute to society without being limited by economic disparities.

SR: Your naivety about socialism's consequences blinds you to the reality of its failures. Look at the atrocities committed by socialist regimes in the past. Fascism recognizes the need for order and security, safeguarding our nation from chaos and external influences that threaten our way of life.

As their arguments clash, the area becomes charged with tension, each assertion reflecting the deeper ideological chasm between them. The discourse embodies the larger struggle between their beliefs, reflecting the historical underpinnings and philosophical contradictions of socialism and fascism.

While Somi thinks of cunning ways to escape, Rajini Reddy stands before a diverse audience, his voice resolute and passionate as he addresses the pressing need for equality in society:

"My fellow comrades, friends, and seekers of justice,

Today, I stand before you not as a father who lost his daughter but as a representative of a collective dream—a dream of a world where every person's worth is not determined by the wealth they possess, but by the content of their character and their contributions to society. A world where the chains of exploitation and oppression are broken, and the light of equality and solidarity shines brightly for all to see.

We live in a world marred by inequality, where a handful of individuals control vast resources while the masses struggle to make ends meet. This unjust distribution of wealth breeds poverty, misery, and the denial of basic human rights. It perpetuates a cycle where the powerful few grow richer while the rest suffer, their potential stifled by circumstances beyond their control.

The assembly seemed appeased by this. Under heavy guard, Somi Reddy was taken to the town hall where hundreds more had gathered for his trial. Rajini himself laid out the landlord's long list of cruel deeds and corruption.

By evening, the people's court had pronounced its swift verdict - confiscation of the Reddy estate lands to be redistributed amongst peasant collectives. And Somi Reddy was sentenced to life imprisonment, spared the noose only by Parvathi's principled intervention. Rajini nodded grimly as the sentence was read out. For once, a powerful oppressor had truly been held accountable. As Somi Reddy was hauled away in chains, the crowd looked to their champion.

But Rajini had disappeared...

He sat alone by the pond where Lakshmi had been laid to rest, tormented by churning thoughts. Part of him knew Parvathi was right - vengeance could never heal his wounded spirit. Another part still pulsed with rage, seeking the total destruction of oppressors like Somi Reddy.

Rajini glanced down at his reflection in the water. For a fleeting moment, the face staring back seemed that of a stranger, twisted by fury and loss. He reeled at what he may have become in his all consuming quest for justice.

Gazing up at the stars, Rajini made a silent vow. I shall not let grief cast me as a mirror to evil. Nor become what I deplore. The righteous struggle continues - but from today, as the man I was born to be. With that, he rose and returned home, where his followers were waiting eagerly. Their champion had rediscovered his moral compass. Rajini Reddy would lead them forward from light, not be consumed by darkness.

Chapter 17
The Rebellion

News of Somi Reddy's dramatic downfall and Rajini's resurgence spread like wildfire across the region. To many, it seemed the first true triumph of the people over generations of exploitation and injustice. Overnight, Rajini became a folk hero, a champion of the oppressed. Songs and stories glorifying his bold defiance of tyranny swirled through village gatherings.

New supporters flocked to join his socialist movement.

But the sober-minded Rajini knew this was just one minor victory. The real struggle still lay ahead to emancipate the masses through systemic change. So, he redoubled his grassroots efforts, re-energized with cautious hope. Rajini led more rallies, spreading awareness of basic rights and urging unity. He expanded community farming collectives where profits were shared equally.

He organized worker cooperatives and credit unions that broke free of debt traps set by rich lenders.

Rajini Reddy's journey from personal tragedy to collective triumph became a pivotal chapter in the history of the struggle against oppression. His ability to channel his grief into action, to turn his pain into purpose, left an indelible mark on the movement. He transformed himself from a grieving individual into a beacon of hope and a symbol of the resilience of the human spirit.

Amidst the rolling hills and fertile plains of Andhra Pradesh, Rajini Reddy's efforts to organize the unorganized were marked by both dedication and creativity. Here are a couple of anecdotes that highlight his innovative approach:

Rajini Reddy: Igniting Hope and Unity

The village itself as a dias, a canvas waited for the master artist to arrive, with fields and houses metaphorically saying welcome.

In a world plagued by inequality and oppression, one man emerged as a beacon of hope for the downtrodden and marginalized.

A huge gathering of peasants and workers in an open field, with Rajini Reddy standing at the front; this scene can give a ray of hope and can scare any oppressor.

Rajini Reddy (Addressing the crowd): My fellow comrades, friends, and seekers of justice,

People's eyes zooming in on Rajini as he speaks passionately.

"Today, we stand at the crossroads of history, where the seeds of change have been sown by our collective yearning for a better future."

The crowd was very attentively listening.

"For too long, we have lived under the shadows of oppression, where a select few have held power over our lives and destinies."

Memories depicting exploitation and struggle unravel in every peasant and worker.

"But I tell you, my friends, that the power to break these chains lies within each and every one of us."

All the eyes of determined farmers looking for a hope in their dark lives.

"We are not mere peasants or workers. We are the backbone of this land, the very foundation upon which society stands."

Peasants unified and working together, raised slogans with their fists punching in the air.

"The time has come to rise, not as individuals, but as a united force against the forces that seek to keep us down.

Look around you. See the faces of your brothers and sisters, those who share your struggles, your dreams, and your aspirations. Our strength lies in our unity. It's time to cast aside the divisions that have held us back and recognize that our destinies are intertwined."

Rajini addressing the entire crowd.

"The rich may have wealth, but we have the power of numbers, the power of solidarity, and the power of our unwavering spirit.

It won't be an easy journey. The road to justice is often filled with obstacles and hardships."

Villagers listening intently, absorbing Rajini's words.

"But remember, my friends, every great change starts with a single step, with a collective decision to rise above fear and oppression.

Let our struggle be a testament to our courage, our resilience, and our unyielding belief in a better world."

The crowd, raising their fists in unity.

"Together, we will overcome, and together, we will build a society where justice, equality, and dignity prevail."

And so, with Rajini Reddy's words as their rallying cry, the peasants and workers embarked on a journey of transformation, united by their shared dreams and the promise of a brighter future.

Chapter 18
The Village of Unity

Rajini went all around where ever there was a need and where ever the oppression prevails. His journey took him to "Gopalapuram" where a loyal follower is about to join him for life.

In a remote village Gopalapuram where the caste system still held a strong grip, Rajini Reddy saw an opportunity to foster unity among the oppressed. He organized a unique event called the "Village of Unity." Peasants from different castes and marginalized workers were invited to participate in a week-long camp.

The camp involved not only political discussions but also cultural exchanges and shared meals. By breaking bread together and engaging in open conversations, barriers began to crumble.

Varada Chary, a skilled carpenter, known for his craftsmanship and dedication to his trade. However, his talents were overshadowed by the oppressive feudal system that dominated his village.

The local landlord Ananda Chakravarthy, whose power was unchecked, exploited Varada Chary and his fellow villagers, subjecting them to heavy taxes and labor without fair compensation. Struggling to make ends meet and witnessing the suffering of his community, Chary began to feel the weight of the feudal chains that bound him. It was a life marked by hardships, fear, and an overwhelming sense of powerlessness.

Rajini Reddy's activism reached Varada Chary's ears like a whisper of hope in a sea of despair. The stories of Rajini's courage, his commitment to justice, and his vision of a better world ignited a spark within Varada's heart. It was as if Rajini's words were a lifeline, offering a way out of the suffocating grip of feudal rule of Chakravarthy.

Intrigued and inspired, Chary sought out Rajini, attending one of his impassioned speeches. He listened with rapt attention as Rajini spoke of solidarity, equality, and the power of collective action. In that moment, Varada saw a glimmer of light at the end of his long tunnel of oppression.

Chary's encounter with Rajini Reddy marked a turning point in his life. He decided to cast aside the role of a victim and embrace the role of a fighter. He became an active participant in Rajini's movement, organizing fellow villagers and educating them about their rights. His skill as a carpenter became a valuable asset, allowing him to contribute to the cause in practical ways, like constructing banners and stages for rallies. As he became more involved, his self-confidence grew.

He realized that his voice mattered, and that together with others, they could challenge the very forces of Chakravarthy that had held them captive for so long. His transformation from a carpenter to a staunch ally of Rajini Reddy exemplified the spirit of the movement—a spirit of empowerment, unity, and the pursuit of justice.

Varada Chary's dedication and resourcefulness caught the attention of Rajini, who recognized his potential as a valuable aide. Chary began to work closely with Rajini, assisting in organizing rallies, disseminating information, and even helping to establish a network of underground activists. His knowledge of the village dynamics, coupled with his newfound confidence, proved to be an asset in advancing the cause of justice.

Chary's journey from a victim of feudalism to an aide of Rajini Reddy symbolized the transformative power of collective action and the unwavering spirit of those who dare to challenge oppressive systems.

Through his determination, he not only liberated himself from the chains of feudalism but also contributed to the larger struggle for a more just and equitable society. His story serves as a reminder that even in the darkest of circumstances, the spark of hope can ignite a fire of change.

As the camp concluded, Rajini proposed a symbolic act: the villagers planted a tree in the village center, signifying their commitment to working together for a brighter future. This event became a turning point, leading to increased collaboration among previously divided groups. The village later became known as a haven of cooperation and solidarity, where the seeds of Rajini's vision took root and flourished.

The British authorities grew increasingly uneasy with Rajini's swelling influence. He had long been a thorn in their side, but they could no longer ignore this rebel who threatened the very economic and social order underpinning imperial rule.

Troop levels were increased to suppress protests and rallies led by Rajini across the province. Those speaking his message were harassed and arrested for sedition.

The British commissioner even tried convincing Parvathi to restrain her husband's activities. This rabble-rousing will only bring him to ruin. You are the only one your husband will heed - convince him to cease this treason, the commissioner warned Parvathi. But Parvathi refused, faithful to Rajini even if she worried for his safety each day. She reminded the British of their own history of rebellion against tyranny. Would your people have gained freedom by acquiescing meekly to their rulers? Our cause is equally just, Parvathi countered.

Meanwhile, Rajini's defiant example was sparking bold new resistance across India. Peasants and workers rose up against exploitative factory and farm owners. Lower castes refused to accept their 'menial' status, emboldened by Rajini's exhortations that all humans are equal.

Students and intellectuals rallied around Rajini, seeing him as a voice of truth and justice. His influence reached even princely states allied with the British, whose subjects were stirred by his passionate call for independence and self determination.

From the Khyber Pass to the Nilgiri Hills, Rajini became a household name. For the timeworn Imperial propaganda portraying Indians as supplicant subjects, he was the resounding counterpoint - a rebel in the cause of liberty.

At a conference in Delhi, the exasperated British viceroy received an earful from loyal princes and landlords. This scoundrel Rajini threatens to ignite revolution across India! His treason must carry the highest penalty! they clamored.

"Rajini is coming to Delhi – Let him come, we should ensure he should not return as the same person"

The viceroy rubbed his furrowed temples vexingly. Rajini had become more than a man - he was an idea. A dangerous idea of defiance and uprising against the mighty British Raj. Trying to eliminate that idea could backfire catastrophically...

Back home, Ramu watched wide-eyed as his father conferred with followers late into the night under flickering oil lamps. He yearned to join the stirring events he could feel swirling around him.

Why can't I go with you on your travels, Father? Ramu asked Rajini one evening. I want to see you make those grand speeches that they all talk about!

Rajini chuckled, but his smile faded as he looked into his son's innocent eyes. I hope your generation will grow up in a free India where such struggle is history. My deepest wish is that you have a childhood unburdened by the weights I bear.

Ramu shook his head vehemently. But I want to fight alongside you, Father! To make you proud...

Rajini kneeled and embraced Ramu. One day I will proudly stand aside as your generation leads India into a bright future. But know this, my son you already make me the proudest father on earth.

Ramu hugged his father tight, sensing the gathering storms ahead. He may have been too young to fully comprehend Rajini's struggle, but in his heart already stirred the rebellious spirit of a young nation seeking freedom.

Chapter 19
The Weavers' Weave of Resistance

The years of struggle were taking their toll on Rajini's health. His endless travels and speeches left him perpetually exhausted. But the growing momentum of the independence movement reenergized his weary spirit. Where once he stirred tentative hopes in isolated pockets, now a churning current of change was sweeping India. Rajini was at the forefront, channeling the swelling aspirations of common people into organised resistance.

In a bustling town dependent on the textile industry, Rajini saw the potential to galvanize a powerful movement. He knew that the weavers held a unique place in the society—they were the backbone of the local economy yet were living in destitution due to exploitative practices. He devised a plan that combined economic empowerment with political awareness.

Rajini encouraged the weavers to collectively demand fair wages and better working conditions. He organized a massive gathering of weavers, where he helped them draft a petition outlining their grievances. To make their voices heard, the weavers embarked on a "Weavers' March" through the town. Each weaver brought a piece of unfinished cloth, which they collectively wove as they walked. This symbolic act illustrated their unity and determination.

As the weavers marched, their movement gained attention and support from other communities. The local authorities were forced to engage in negotiations, and through persistence and unwavering solidarity, the weavers achieved some of their demands. This victory not only improved their lives but also demonstrated the power of organized action and inspired workers across different sectors to join the growing resistance against oppressive forces.

Peasants and laborers increasingly rallied around his socialist vision of an equitable society. His message of empowerment resonated from the poorest villages to universities. A broad-based struggle for home rule under the unifying banner of the Indian National Congress party was looking for leaders like Rajini.

The Story of Yadagiri

In a village near Kalinga region where power was concentrated in the hands of a few, Somanatha Prachanda, Sarva Rayudu, Bala Mahapatra, and their gang wielded their authority with unchecked power, causing instability and turmoil that cast a dark shadow over the entire society. In the heart of a village scarred by caste discrimination and feudal oppression, the story of Yadagiri emerged as a testament to the resilience of the human spirit. A Dalit man, he had suffered the cruelest fate imaginable – his family torn apart by the lust and tyranny of the feudal lords who held their lives in contempt.

Reign of Fear and Exploitation

Somanatha Prachanda, Sarva Rayudu, Bala Mahapatra, and their gang saw themselves as the rulers of the village. With their wealth and influence, they exploited their position to create a climate of fear and oppression. They used their unchecked power to extract resources, impose heavy taxes, and manipulate the lives of the villagers to their advantage.

The gang's domination extended beyond economic exploitation. They controlled vital resources, businesses, and industries, leaving the villagers at their mercy. Through manipulation and intimidation, they extracted exorbitant profits, leaving the working class struggling to survive while the gang prospered.

Anyone who dared to question their authority or challenge their methods faced dire consequences. The gang's enforcers silenced dissent through threats, violence, and coercion. The villagers watched in fear as those who spoke out were targeted, their lives turned into cautionary tales of what happened to those who dared oppose the gang's power.

As the gang's grip tightened, the once harmonious society descended into chaos. The villagers lived in constant uncertainty, their dreams and aspirations crushed under the weight of oppression. Fear permeated the air, choking the voices of those who longed for justice and change.

The gang's actions eroded the values that held the community together. Trust and unity dissolved, replaced by suspicion and apathy. Neighbors became wary of one another, afraid to form alliances or speak out against the atrocities they witnessed.

Families like Yadagiri's suffered the collateral damage of the gang's tyranny. Their lives were shattered, their dignity torn apart, as the gang wielded their power without consequence. The village watched in despair, feeling powerless to protect their own. Yadagiri's life was shattered when the powerful feudal lords of his village took advantage of their unchecked authority.

His family, marginalized and vulnerable due to their Dalit identity, became the target of their cruelty. His loved ones were torn away, leaving Yadagiri with nothing but the scars of a tragedy that seemed insurmountable. Yadagiri's family, once a source of comfort and love, tragically became victims of the oppressive feudal system that ruled their village. Their story was one of resilience in the face of cruelty and a catalyst for his unwavering determination to fight for justice.

Yadagiri's family lived in a simple but peaceful home, surrounded by fields that they tended with care. Their dwelling, while modest, was a haven of love, unity, and shared dreams. In the embrace of their family, they found solace from the challenges they faced as Dalits in a caste-divided society.

Yadagiri's family was rooted in the values of hard work, unity, and the simple joys of life. His parents, with their unwavering support, taught him to face life's challenges with dignity and perseverance. His siblings, close in age and spirit, were his companions in both laughter and shared responsibilities.

As the feudal lords exercised their unchecked power, Yadagiri's family found themselves trapped in a nightmare. The lords saw Yadagiri's family as nothing more than pawns to satisfy their desires and further their dominion. Despite their modest existence, the family's Dalit identity made them vulnerable targets of the feudal lords' cruelty.

The fateful day that forever changed Yadagiri's life began like any other, with the sun rising over the village and casting its warm glow on the homes and fields. But beneath the surface of this seemingly ordinary day lurked the shadows of oppression and cruelty that would shatter Yadagiri's world.

As the day progressed, a sense of foreboding settled over the village. The feudal lords, a powerful and entitled group who had dominated the lives of the villagers for generations, arrived with an air of arrogance. Their presence cast a pall over the village, a reminder of the unchecked authority they wielded.

The sun began its descent, and with it, the nightmare began to unfold. The feudal lords, fueled by their lust for power and their disregard for human dignity, set their sights on Yadagiri's family. They stormed into their home, their actions devoid of empathy or humanity. What transpired within the walls of

Yadagiri's home was a grotesque violation of the sanctity of family and humanity.

The feudal lords inflicted unimaginable pain, their actions driven by their lust and their disregard for the lives they were destroying. Yadagiri's loved ones, innocent victims of this cruelty, were torn apart from each other, leaving behind a trail of heartbreak and despair.

As the sun dipped below the horizon, it cast long shadows over the village that mirrored the darkness that had befallen his family. The aftermath of the feudal lords' actions left Yadagiri grappling with a pain that defied description. His once-close-knit family had been burnt into ashes after a brutal sexual assault. In the aftermath of this tragedy, his spirit was tested to its limits.

He was left with an emptiness that seemed insurmountable, a grief that threatened to consume him. The fateful day left his heart and spirit wounded, but it also ignited a spark within him – a spark of resistance, of determination to fight against the forces that had torn his family apart. Though his family had been taken from him by the cruelty of the feudal lords, their memory lived on in his tireless activism.

His commitment to justice became a testament to their strength and the strength of countless others who had suffered. He channeled his grief into action, using his pain to fuel his determination to bring an end to the cycle of oppression.

Through his efforts, he sought to ensure that no family would be subjected to the same fate, and that the legacy of his loved ones would be one of resilience, transformation, and hope for a better future. It became the driving force behind his alliance with Rajini Reddy and his commitment to seek justice, not just for his own family, but for all those who had suffered under the oppressive rule of the feudal lords.

The fateful day marked the beginning of Yadagiri's journey from victim to fighter, from sorrow to resilience, and from darkness to a beacon of hope for a better tomorrow. The words and actions of Rajini Reddy, the socialist activist who had been stirring the embers of resistance, reached Yadagiri's ears.

Rajini's message of equality, justice, and empowerment resonated deeply with Yadagiri's wounded soul.

He started attending meetings, discussions, and rallies organized by Rajini's movement. Slowly but steadily, Yadagiri found himself shedding the cloak of silence and invisibility that society had imposed upon him. He discovered the power of collective action and the strength that came from standing alongside others who had been marginalized and oppressed.

The atrocities committed by the gang served as a catalyst for a grassroots movement to rise. As the villagers banded together, they faced their fears and dared to challenge the gang's supremacy. Through collective action, they aimed to dismantle the unjust power structures that had kept them oppressed.

The battle for justice was fraught with challenges, but the villagers' determination and resilience began to chip away at the gang's dominance.

Rajini's unwavering belief in the power of unity and the potential for change ignited a spark within him. This spark, born from the depths of his pain, began to grow into a flame of determination. His journey wasn't just one of personal transformation; it was a contribution to a larger fight for justice. His deep empathy for those who had suffered as he had fueled his determination to make a difference.

He became an advocate for the oppressed, using his voice to raise awareness about the atrocities committed by the feudal lords and the urgent need for change. His presence became a symbol of resistance, a living embodiment of the spirit that refused to be broken by adversity.

Individuals like Yadagiri and Rajini Reddy refused to bow to the gang's oppression. They recognized that unchecked power would lead to the destruction of their society and were determined to kindle the flames of change.

Chapter 20
A Movement Is Born

Through Rajini's leadership and Yadagiri's unwavering resolve, the villagers slowly began to find their voices again. The gang's rule may have been harsh, but it couldn't extinguish the human spirit's yearning for justice and freedom.

He stood side by side with Rajini Reddy and countless others who had refused to be defeated by the cruelty of their circumstances. Through their collective efforts, they forged a path towards a more just and equitable society – a society where the Yadagiris of the world could rise from the ashes, not as victims, but as victors of their own destinies. However, even in the darkest of times, a flicker of resistance remained.

Rajini alongside Yadagiri, Varada chary and many others marched towards the police station seeking justice regarding the atrocities committed by the gang. The British police seemed least bothered and warned the villagers that they would open fire and kill as many as possible, with that word, some of the aggressive villagers almost tore down the Police station. They were stopped by a word from Rajini's mouth.

Rajini told the Police inspector,

"Officer! You just have witnessed what a revolted individuals can do. We demand for the arrest of Prachanda and his gang for the atrocities they committed, and they should be sentenced to life for the numerous lives they have destroyed.

All the property they have snatched should be returned to the rightful people. All this should be done by the dusk. If not, I won't stop the people from tearing down you all and the gang."

Fearing an out break of a civil disobedience and a peasant war, the Police sought the help of higher authorities. The higher authorities were in a different mind game and asked the Inspector to do as Rajini says. Everything that Rajini had asked for was done and the people were joyous and started celebrating their triumph over oppression.

The police have arrested the gang even after the resistance from the henchmen, even the henchmen of the gang was also imprisoned while some of them fled away from the scene.

In this tale of oppression, fear, and resistance, the actions of Somanatha Prachanda and gang served as a sobering reminder of the consequences of unchecked power. But it was also a story of the indomitable human spirit, capable of rising from the depths of despair to challenge the darkest of forces in the pursuit of a more just and equitable society.

Meanwhile, at a climate conference in Shimla, the British viceroy was berated by fellow imperial officials for letting the unrest fester.

"You've allowed native agitation to gain dangerous traction!" the blustery South African delegate accused. "If these unruly elements are not crushed immediately, untold calamity will befall the Empire."

"We have a plan and that black dog will not leave Delhi unharmed!"roared the British officer.

The viceroy interlaced his fingers contemplatively before responding. "Heavy-handed suppression will only increase their allure as righteous rebels. We must instead dilute this movement's fervor through divisions and moderation." So British officials sought to fracture the independence coalition by stoking Hindu-Muslim tensions. They also propped up their own moderate collaborators to replace firebrands like Rajini at the helm of the freedom struggle.

In the meanwhile, Rajini came to Delhi to attend a conference of INC to make them listen to his voice. Some of the leaders were jealous about the Massive people support Rajini got and tried to sideline him by not giving him chance to speak. But Rajini was not so easily sidelined.

He continued touring the countryside, whipping up nationalist passion through his rousing oratory. To counter the British propaganda, Rajini spoke of unity, appealing to common values that transcended religious differences.

On his tour, he stayed in an open field roadside along with the thousands who were marching with him. A man in his early thirties, in soiled clothes and wearing broken spectacles, was seen moving suspiciously, Varada chary had a doubt whether this person has come to assassinate Rajini. He went to Ravi and told his suspicion.

Ravi along with Varada chary, Yadagiri and other followers held the suspicious man by arm before he could react and brought him to Rajini. Rajini asked his followers to free the man and offered him some water and food.

The man gulped the food at one go and started coughing. With a kind heart, Rajini patted on his head. The man started crying and said, "What they say is right! You are a gem of a man! What they is right!"

The man started sobbing.

Rajini soothed him and asked "What is your name and what is your story dear brother?"

The man told "My name is Rajan." He shared his story which moved Rajini very much.

Chapter 21
A Battle for Education

In the heart of rural India near Delhi, there is a village Kalapur and there lived a man named Bhola, a Dalit father with an unyielding dream. He was determined to break free from the chains of caste discrimination and provide his son, Rajan, with the education that was denied to him and his ancestors for generations.

Bhola's life had been an unending cycle of hardship and humiliation.

His family, like many others in their community, worked as agricultural laborers, eking out a meager existence while enduring daily insults and discrimination. But Bhola was different; he possessed an insatiable thirst for knowledge, a fire in his heart that refused to be extinguished.

Rumors had spread of a school run by a progressive teacher named "Shivendu Sharma" in a neighboring village.

Bhola believed that this school held the key to Rajan's future. With determination etched in his eyes, he approached Mr. Sharma and made a heartfelt plea for Rajan's admission. Moved by Bhola's unwavering resolve, Mr. Sharma agreed to admit Rajan with one condition: Bhola would have to work in the fields overviewing agriculture to pay for his son's higher education.

Sharma's intention was to provide employment to the poor father. He wanted Bhola to generate money for Rajan's higher education which is very expensive. He taught Rajan for free, but that has to look as exploitation in the high society, as some part of the society was not ready to accept Dalit's alongside them equally.

Bhola accepted the challenge with open arms, knowing that the road ahead would be arduous. He toiled day in and day out under the scorching sun, his blistered hands tilling the land and planting seeds. Every grain of rice harvested and every bundle of hay cut was a step closer to Rajan's higher education.

Life was far from easy for Bhola's family. They lived in a humble thatched-roof hut on the outskirts of the village. The upper-caste villagers did everything in their power to maintain the status quo.

They withheld water from Dalit homes, spat on their paths, and refused to interact with them in any meaningful way. Bhola's wife, Gita, faced her own battles, working as a maid in an upper-caste household to supplement their meager income.

But amidst the adversity, Bhola and Gita maintained their unwavering resolve. Their focus was singular: to ensure Rajan's education. Often, they gathered under the dim light of an oil lamp in their humble home, where Rajan would read aloud from the few books they had managed to acquire.

Bhola would listen intently, though he couldn't understand most of what Rajan was learning. Nevertheless, he knew that education was the key to breaking the cycle of oppression, and he was determined to provide his son with that key.

Years passed, and Rajan grew into a bright and diligent young boy. His dedication to his studies was unparalleled, and Mr. Sharma recognized his potential. Rajan's progress was undeniable, and the village began to take notice. The upper-caste families, who once treated the Dalits with disdain, started to see Rajan as a threat to the established order.

One evening, as Rajan returned home from school, he was confronted by a group of upper-caste boys. They taunted him, calling him derogatory names and demanding that he stop going to school.

Rajan, though frightened, stood his ground. He knew that his education was not just for himself but for his entire community. His courage impressed the bullies, and they soon realized that Rajan was not to be deterred.

Word of Rajan's bravery reached Mr. Sharma, who decided to take a bold step. He organized a meeting with the villagers, including the upper-caste families, to discuss the importance of education for all children, regardless of caste.

He spoke eloquently about the need for social change and the benefits of an educated society. While some were resistant to change, others began to see the wisdom in his words.

Bhola also spoke at the meeting. His voice trembled with emotion as he recounted the sacrifices he and his family had made. He implored the villagers to support Rajan's education, not just for their sake but for the entire village's future.

Slowly, hearts began to change. The realization that education was a universal right began to take hold. The upper-caste families, some out of genuine conviction and others out of fear of being ostracized by the changing times, began to send their own children to school alongside Rajan.

This transformation did not happen overnight, and there were still challenges to overcome.

Chapter 22
The Inevitable

The Dalit families continued to face discrimination, but the seed of change had been planted. As more and more children from different castes sat side by side in the classroom, the walls of prejudice began to crumble.

Years Passed...

Rajan completed his school education and pursued higher studies in the city with the help of financial savings Bhola had generated with the help of Mr.Sharma. He returned to Kalapur as a well-educated man. His journey had been arduous, but it had been made possible by the unwavering determination of his father, Bhola, and the support of his teacher, Mr. Sharma.

Rajan's return marked a turning point for the village. He started working in the school along with Mr. Sharma, dedicated to providing education to all children, regardless of their caste or background. The school quickly gained popularity, and Rajan's vision of an educated and united village began to take shape.

Over time, as more and more children received an education, the community transformed. The old prejudices and divisions slowly faded away, replaced by a sense of unity and shared purpose. The village of Kalapur became a model of social progress and change, a testament to what could be achieved when people came together to challenge injustice and inequality.

Bhola, who had sacrificed so much for his son's education, lived to see the transformation of his village. He passed away peacefully, knowing that he had played a vital role in breaking the chains of caste discrimination. His legacy lived on through his son, Rajan, who continued to champion the cause of education and social equality throughout his life.

But just when it seemed that the story was reaching its long-awaited climax, an unexpected and bitter twist unfolded. A group of powerful and influential feudal lords from the neighboring villages saw Rajan's school as a threat to their control over the Dalit labor force.

These feudal lords held sway over vast expanses of land and had a stranglehold on the livelihoods of the Dalit families. They feared that an educated Dalit population would demand better wages, fair treatment, and, ultimately, freedom from the bonds of servitude. In their eyes, an educated Dalit population posed a direct challenge to their dominance.

One fateful day, as Rajan was teaching a group of eager students in the makeshift school, armed men sent by the feudal lords stormed into the village. They carried out a brutal and swift raid, destroying the school, burning books, and beating anyone who tried to resist. Rajan and Mr. Sharma, who had stood with the Dalit community, were mercilessly beaten and left injured.

The Dalit families were left in a state of shock and terror. The feudal lords made it clear that any attempt to educate Dalit children would be met with violent reprisals. The message was clear: they would do whatever it took to maintain their grip on power.

Bhola, who had sacrificed his health and worked tirelessly to provide Rajan with an education, felt a profound sense of despair. His dream of a brighter future for his community had been shattered, and the hope that had sustained him for so long was extinguished.

In the face of such overwhelming power and brutality, the villagers had no choice but to bow down to the feudal lords' demands. The school was never rebuilt, and the children, including Rajan, were forced to abandon their pursuit of education.

The story of Bhola, Rajan, and the village of Kalapur serves as a poignant reminder of the entrenched injustices that plagued India in the early 1900s. Despite the Dalit community's unwavering determination and the progress they had made, the oppressive forces of feudalism and caste discrimination proved too formidable to overcome.

The anti-climax serves as a stark reminder that the fight for social justice and equality is often met with formidable obstacles, and progress can be painfully slow. However, it also underscores the resilience and determination of individuals like Bhola, Rajan, and Mr. Sharma, who, against all odds, dared to challenge the status quo and planted the seeds of change, even if they were not able to see their dreams fully realized. Their story remains a living proof to the enduring struggle for a more just and equitable society.

As Rajan and his community faced the devastating setback of the brutal raid by the feudal lords, hope seemed all but lost. The flames of their dreams for education had been extinguished, and the villagers were left in despair.

It was at this critical juncture that Rajan decided to seek help from an unexpected source – a renowned social reformer and champion of Dalit rights named Rajini Kantha.

Rajini Kantha was a well-known figure in the region, known for his tireless efforts to uplift the oppressed and marginalized communities. He had successfully challenged the oppressive caste system in various villages and had even faced threats to his life. But his dedication to the cause of social justice remained unshaken.

Rajan traveled to a nearby town where Rajini Kantha was known to reside. He was determined to seek the help and guidance of this influential figure. It was a long and arduous journey, but Rajan's unwavering resolve fueled his determination.

Upon reaching the town, Rajan asked around and eventually found his way to Rajini Kantha's modest home. But he was not there, then he set on the journey till he reached the place where he is now and expressed out the story of his village, the raid, and the desperate need for education.

Rajini Kantha was deeply moved by the plight of Rajan's community. He knew that the battle for social justice was a long and difficult one, often fraught with setbacks. However, he also believed that the spirit of resilience and determination could overcome even the most formidable obstacles.

Chapter 23
A Promise Made

With a sense of purpose, Rajini Kantha decided to visit Kalapur and meet the villagers personally. He knew that his presence and advocacy could draw attention to their cause and put pressure on the feudal lords to relent. But he also understood the risks involved, as his actions often drew the ire of those who sought to maintain the status quo.

Rajini Kantha arrived in Kalapur to a warm welcome from the Dalit families. His presence ignited a spark of hope in their hearts, a glimmer of possibility in the face of overwhelming adversity. He spoke passionately to the villagers, encouraging them to stand firm in their quest for education and equality.

Aware of the dangers posed by the feudal lords, Rajini Kantha also used his influence to garner support from sympathetic individuals and organizations. He reached out to other social reformers, activists, and even journalists, urging them to shine a spotlight on the injustice faced by the villagers of Kalapur.

News of Rajini Kantha's involvement in the struggle spread like wildfire. It drew the attention of not only local media but also concerned citizens from across the region. Pressure mounted on the feudal lords to reconsider their oppressive stance. They began to feel the weight of public opinion turning against them.

Rajini Kantha's efforts bore fruit as negotiations were initiated between the Dalit community and the feudal lords. With the support of sympathetic parties and the fear of public backlash, a compromise was reached. The feudal lords agreed to allow the resumption of the village school, provided it operated with certain restrictions.

While it was not a complete victory, it was a significant step forward. The school was reopened, and Rajan, along with other children from the Dalit community, could once again pursue their education. It was a moment of triumph, a testament to the power of collective action and the unwavering determination of individuals like Rajini Kantha and Rajan.

As the school doors swung open once more, the villagers of Kalapur felt a renewed sense of hope. They knew that the path to equality was long and fraught with challenges, but they were determined to walk it with their heads held high. Rajini Kantha's intervention had given them a second chance at realizing their dreams, and they were not going to let it slip away.

Rajan, whose dreams had been briefly shattered, resumed his school with even greater determination. He was inspired not only by his father, Bhola, and his teacher, Mr. Sharma, but also by the selfless efforts of Rajini Kantha and the solidarity of his community. He knew that education was not just a personal pursuit; it was a means to challenge injustice and create a more equitable society.

The Speech

Rajini Kantha gives a goosebumps speech to unite the dalit community againist the feudal forces to fight for their education, which is their right and can change their fate.

Under the scorching sun, in the heart of Kalapur village, a gathering had been arranged. The Dalit community, who had faced discrimination and oppression for far too long, had come together once more. Among them stood Rajini Kantha, the renowned social reformer who had taken up their cause, his presence commanding the attention of all.

As the villagers settled, the air was thick with a mixture of hope and apprehension. The recent events, the reopening of their school, had given them a renewed sense of purpose. Yet, the looming threat of the feudal forces, who sought to maintain their dominance, cast a shadow over their hopes.

Rajini Kantha stepped forward, his voice unwavering and powerful, echoing through the gathered crowd. His words carried the weight of conviction, and he spoke with a passion that resonated with every heart in the village.

"My brothers and sisters of Kalapur," he began, "I stand before you today not as a savior but as a fellow traveler on the path of justice.

Our struggle is not an easy one, and the road ahead is fraught with challenges. But remember this: the strength of our unity can overcome even the mightiest of oppressors."

He paused, letting his words sink in, his eyes scanning the faces before him, filled with determination.

"Our ancestors endured centuries of injustice and discrimination, and we carry the weight of that history on our shoulders. But today, we have the opportunity to change the course of our destiny. The school that we fought so hard to reopen is not just a place of learning; it is a symbol of our resistance, a beacon of hope for future generations."

The crowd nodded in agreement, their resolve growing with each word.

"Education is the key that can unlock the chains that have bound us for generations. It is the weapon with which we can fight back against the forces that seek to keep us in servitude.

But remember, knowledge is not power until it is shared, until it is used to uplift our entire community."

Rajini Kantha's words hung in the air, heavy with meaning. He continued, "The feudal forces may be powerful, but they are not invincible. They fear our unity, our determination, and our collective strength. They seek to divide us, to break our spirit, but we shall not yield."

A murmur of agreement rippled through the crowd, and some faces that had borne expressions of doubt now sparkled with newfound hope.

Rajini Kantha raised his voice, his words ringing out with even greater intensity. "We are not just fighting for our own rights; we are fighting for the rights of every Dalit, every marginalized soul in this land. Our struggle today will be remembered by generations to come. Our children and their children should inherit a world where discrimination is but a distant memory."

He pointed towards the school building in the distance, its doors once again open to the eager minds of Dalit children. "Let that school be a testament to our determination, a symbol of our defiance. Let every book in that school be a weapon in our battle against ignorance and oppression."

The crowd stood in silence, their hearts swelling with pride and determination. Rajini Kantha's speech had ignited a fire within them, a fire that would not be extinguished. They knew that the road ahead would be difficult, that they would face threats and challenges, but they were united by a common purpose – the pursuit of education, justice, and equality.

As the gathering dispersed, the villagers of Kalapur carried with them the words of Rajini Kantha, a rallying cry that would serve as a constant reminder of their shared mission. They were ready to face the feudal forces, to stand up against oppression, and to continue the fight for their right to education.

And so, the struggle continued, with renewed vigor and a sense of unity that transcended caste and creed. Rajini Kantha's speech had breathed new life into their cause, and they were determined to carry the torch of justice forward, no matter the obstacles they encountered. The battle was far from over, but with their hearts united, they believed that victory was not only possible but inevitable.

Chapter 24
The Feudal - British Alliance

Brijesh Thakur and his son Anoop Thakur, as they sided with the British colonial rulers in their divisive politics, creating anarchy in Kalapur.

In the early 1900s, Kalapur was a village trapped in a web of oppressive traditions and the entrenched caste system that defined Indian society during British colonial rule. At the heart of this village, Brijesh Thakur and his son Anoop Thakur wielded immense power and influence.

Brijesh Thakur was a wealthy and cunning landowner who had managed to amass vast expanses of land and resources over the years. His wealth and status were deeply tied to his collaboration with the British colonial authorities. He saw the British as protectors of his interests, even if it meant upholding the oppressive caste system and exploiting the labor of the Dalit community.

Anoop Thakur, the son, was a shrewd and Western-educated individual who had imbibed the values of the colonial education system. He presented himself as a progressive leader, often playing both sides – outwardly supporting the British agenda while secretly working to undermine the aspirations of the oppressed communities in the village.

The Thakurs, like many other feudal lords of the time, recognized the benefits of collaborating with the British rulers. They willingly embraced the British policy of "divide and rule." Their objective was to create an atmosphere of division, mistrust, and anarchy within the village to protect their own interests.

To achieve this, they employed a series of manipulative tactics:

Exploiting Caste Divisions: The Thakurs played upon the existing caste divisions within the village. They used their influence to pit different castes against each other, exacerbating tensions and animosities that had existed for generations.

Rumormongering: They spread malicious rumors and misinformation, sowing seeds of mistrust among the villagers. False stories about one group plotting against another were a common tool in their arsenal.

Diverting Attention: The Thakurs encouraged conflicts and rivalries over trivial matters to divert the villagers' attention away from larger issues, such as education and social equality.

Manipulating Religious Differences: They exploited religious differences, stoking communal tensions within the village. They attempted to turn one religious community against another, creating further divisions.

Bribing and Coercion: The Thakurs used their wealth and resources to buy the loyalty of some villagers and intimidate others into submission. This created an atmosphere of fear and uncertainty.

The result of these tactics was an atmosphere of chaos and anarchy in Kalapur. The villagers were divided, suspicious of one another, and often engaged in petty conflicts that served the Thakurs' interests by preventing any meaningful collective action.

The Thakurs, driven by their self-serving agenda, sought to undermine the unity of the villagers of Kalapur. They used their influence and resources to fuel divisions within the community, exploiting existing fault lines of caste and religion. They instigated conflicts and rivalries, pitting different groups against each other to divert attention from the common cause of education and equality.

They spread rumors and misinformation, sowing seeds of mistrust and animosity among the villagers. In their divisive politics, they tried to turn caste against caste, neighbor against neighbor, and friend against friend. Their ultimate goal was to weaken the resolve of the Dalit community and crush their aspirations for a better future.

Anoop Thakur, in particular, was known for his cunning and manipulative tactics. He used his education and Westernized outlook to portray himself as a progressive leader while secretly working against the very principles of justice and equality that Rajini Kantha and the villagers stood for. He collaborated with the British authorities to suppress dissent and ensure that the Dalit community remained subservient.

The Thakurs' alliance with the British not only perpetuated the caste-based oppression but also created an atmosphere of anarchy and instability in the region. They were willing to sacrifice the well-being and aspirations of their own people for personal gain and power. Their actions were a stark reminder of how the colonial powers often relied on opportunistic collaborators to maintain control over their subjects, hence creating anarchy.

It was within this fractured and tumultuous environment that the arrival of Rajini Kantha would prove to be a turning point. His commitment to justice, his ability to unify the community, and his determination to challenge the divisive politics of the Thakurs would ultimately reshape the fate of Kalapur. But before this transformation could occur, the villagers would have to confront the Thakurs and their insidious tactics head-on, a formidable challenge in its own right.

Despite the Thakurs' efforts to sow discord and anarchy, the villagers of Kalapur, under the leadership of Rajini, remained resolute. They recognized the Thakurs' divisive tactics for what they were – a desperate attempt to maintain their grip on power. The unity forged by Rajini's impassioned speeches and unwavering commitment to justice proved stronger than the Thakurs' divisive politics.

The battle for education and equality in Kalapur was not just a fight against the British colonial system but also a struggle against the forces of oppression within their own community. It was a test of resilience and determination in the face of formidable adversaries like Brijesh Thakur and Anoop Thakur, who were willing to compromise their own people's well-being for their personal gain.

The simmering tension between the oppressed Dalit community and the oppressive feudal lords, Brijesh Thakur and his son Anoop Thakur, finally reached a boiling point in the village of Kalapur. The villagers had endured years of exploitation, division, and injustice at the hands of the Thakurs, who had allied themselves with the British colonial authorities to maintain their power.

Rajini left the village in the middle of night to a near by town to attend a secret meeting of some radical youth who were planning some attacks on the British court.

Chapter 25
Flares and Smoke

It's been a week already, the villagers unified and tasted the success by making the thakur's go on backfoot in the school's issue. They wanted a permanent solution. But Rajan told the villagers to wait until Rajini comes, but they thought it will be too late. They wanted to strike while the iron is hot.

One fateful day, Rajan and the villagers, driven by desperation and a burning desire for justice, decided to take matters into their own hands. They gathered in secret, away from the prying eyes of the Thakurs and their henchmen, and devised a plan to confront the oppressors who had held them in bondage for far too long.

Under the cover of darkness, the villagers, led by Rajan and other fearless individuals, marched toward the Thakurs' imposing bungalow, which had long been a symbol of their tyranny. They were armed not with weapons, but with the sheer force of their collective will and an unwavering determination to end the cycle of oppression.

The attack on the Thakurs' bungalow was swift and relentless. The villagers, driven by a burning desire for justice and equality, tore down the gates and stormed into the estate. Their anger was palpable, and their determination unshakable.

The Thakurs and their henchmen, taken by surprise, attempted to defend their fortress of privilege. But the villagers, united in their cause, overwhelmed them with sheer numbers and the intensity of their resolve. It was a battle not of physical strength, but of the unyielding spirit of a community that had endured far too much.

The bungalow that had once stood as a symbol of the Thakurs' power and oppression was reduced to ruins. Its walls crumbled, its opulent furnishings lay in ruins, and the very foundation of their authority was shattered.

The Thakurs and their henchmen, who had for so long exercised unchecked authority, found themselves at the mercy of the villagers they had oppressed. In a moment of poetic justice, they were tied to a tree, hanging upside down, a cruel form of punishment that had been inflicted upon the Dalits countless times.

The act served as a powerful message – a reversal of the power dynamic that had defined their lives for so long. The Thakurs, who had used their influence and authority to subjugate the Dalit community, were now subjected to a taste of their own medicine.

As they hung there, humbled and defeated, they were forced to confront the consequences of their actions. The villagers did not seek revenge but rather justice and equality. They wanted the Thakurs to understand the pain and suffering they had caused and to acknowledge the need for change.

The events of that night marked a turning point in Kalapur's history. The Thakurs, once untouchable in their power, had been brought to their knees by the collective will of the villagers. It was a moment that symbolized the triumph of justice over oppression and unity over division.

In the aftermath, the villagers, having made their point, released the Thakurs, but not before extracting a promise from them to abandon the village and their oppressive ways and support the cause of education and equality. The Thakurs, now aware of the consequences of their actions, reluctantly agreed.

The Thakurs forcibly redirected their resources toward the betterment of the entire village, supporting initiatives for education and social equality. All the property was distributed to the rightful owners and peasants. But they were waiting for the right opportunity to strike back this time very meticulously planned.

As news of the villagers' daring act against the Thakurs spread, it inevitably caught the attention of the British colonial authorities. The Thakurs, who had long enjoyed a cozy relationship with the colonial administration, wasted no time in appealing for assistance. In response, a contingent of British police officers was dispatched to Kalapur to "restore order" and "protect British interests."

The arrival of the British police was met with a mixture of fear and determination among the villagers. They knew that their actions against the Thakurs had consequences, and the might of the colonial power was not to be underestimated.

The police arrived in Kalapur with stern faces and orders to restore "law and order." They demanded that the villagers disperse and allow them to take control of the situation. But the villagers, who had tasted a momentary victory against oppression, were not willing to back down without a fight.

A standoff ensued, with the villagers forming a human barricade to protect their homes and their newfound sense of justice. They chanted slogans of equality and waved placards demanding their right to education and freedom from oppression.

Tensions escalated as neither side was willing to yield. The British police officers, feeling threatened by the villagers' defiance, began to raise their rifles in a show of force. It was a powder keg waiting to explode, with anger, fear, and determination swirling in the air.

In a moment of chaos and confusion, a single gunshot rang out. It's unclear who fired the first shot, but it triggered a hail of bullets as the police officers opened fire on the villagers. Panic and chaos erupted as villagers scattered in all directions, seeking cover from the sudden onslaught.

Amidst the chaos, tragedy struck. Some villagers were injured by the gunfire, and in the crossfire, several police officers were also hit. The situation rapidly escalated into a tragic and deadly confrontation.

In the aftermath, the Thakurs, who had sought refuge with the British police, did not emerge unscathed. The very authority they had relied on to protect their interests had inadvertently turned into their executioners. In the crossfire, Brijesh Thakur and his son Anoop

Thakur lost their lives, their once-powerful influence brought to a brutal end.

Five white policemen also lost their lives in the confrontation, and the village of Kalapur was left in a state of shock and mourning. The events that had transpired were a stark reminder of the high stakes involved in the fight for justice and equality during colonial rule.

Chapter 26
The Shock Waves

The tragic incident sent shockwaves through the British administration, which now faced the challenge of quelling the unrest in Kalapur and maintaining control over the situation. It also drew the attention of the wider world, as the events in Kalapur became a symbol of the broader struggle for independence and justice in colonial India.

The villagers, grieving their losses, continued their fight for education and equality, now with the added weight of the lives lost during the confrontation. Their struggle had exacted a heavy toll, but their determination remained unbroken.

In the aftermath of the tragic confrontation in Kalapur, where the villagers had lost their newfound leaders, the Thakurs, and several police officers, a sense of defiance and unity continued to course through the community. The villagers were no longer willing to bow down to oppression, and they were determined to reclaim their true freedom.

Fueled by a renewed spirit of resistance, the villagers gathered in large numbers, their collective will stronger than ever. They decided to confront the remaining British police officers who had not been injured or killed in the earlier exchange.

With shouts of determination, the villagers confronted the police contingent, demanding that they leave Kalapur and never return. They surrounded the officers, who, faced with the fierce resolve of the villagers, eventually retreated from the village, beaten and humiliated.

As the police officers left Kalapur, the villagers celebrated their hard-won victory. It was a moment of triumph over oppression, a moment that would be remembered for generations to come.

However, their act of defiance did not come without consequences.

The British colonial authorities were not ones to tolerate insubordination. They saw the events in Kalapur as a challenge to their authority and a threat to the stability of their rule. The British actually staged the firing to eradicate Rajini, but it was missed as he was not in the village at the time of event. The villagers chase away the remaining police men out of their village and reclaim their true freedom, but this sows seed to the arrest of Rajini reddy.

Word of the confrontation quickly spread beyond the village, reaching the ears of the British authorities. They saw an opportunity to make an example of someone, to quell any further dissent, and to reassert their dominance.

In their eyes, Rajini Reddy, the charismatic leader who had rallied the villagers and inspired their defiance, was the face of the rebellion. His impassioned speeches and unwavering commitment to justice had made him a symbol of hope for the villagers, but also a target for the British authorities.

One day, as Rajini was returning to the village after knowing about the tragic event, he was ambushed by British police officers. They arrested him, charging him with incitement, sedition, and rebellion against colonial authority in kalapur.

The news of Rajini's arrest sent shockwaves through the village. The villagers were now faced with the harsh reality of their actions. They had reclaimed their freedom from the Thakurs and the police, but it had come at a great cost.

Rajini, the beacon of their struggle, was now imprisoned, and his fate hung in the balance. The villagers were torn between grief and anger, knowing that their fight for justice was far from over.

As Rajini awaited trial, the villagers rallied behind him, determined to secure his release and continue the fight for education, equality, and freedom. They knew that their struggle was not just about one leader; it was about the collective will of a community that refused to be silenced, a community that had tasted the sweet taste of freedom and would stop at nothing to protect it.

All the people started worrying about the safety of Rajini, as they does not have any legal support. But Rajini himself is a barrister who took up his own case and argued. He called Ravi and Varadha chary and told them to do something. He met the other leaders who were arrested and told them that they will be set free very soon.

In the twisting and turning events of the court trail, with the entire court and police waiting for the death sentence of Rajini, there unfurled an event which shocked everyone. An alibi of Rajini was proved in the court by another court official who testified that Rajini was present in the town's court when the incident took place in Kalapur.

The official added that, it is Rajini who stopped the aggressive youth from bombing the court complex, Rajini believes in peace and equality unless the situations are extreme. So this disproves the conspiracy. As the court official of that higher rank testified, there is no other way except to release him and drop off all charges.

The official was called to the court by Ravi and Varadha who executed Rajini's plan flawlessly.

Kalapur, once divided and oppressed, began to transform into a community where justice prevailed, and unity thrived. The villagers, fueled by the spirit of their struggle and their unwavering commitment to education, worked together to build a brighter future for themselves and generations to come. Their aggressive step destabilized their safety a bit but with mature leaders like Rajini and Rajan, they could claim their righteous place.

Chapter 27
Rajini Comes Home After the Release

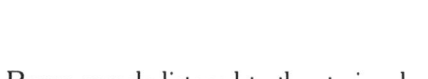

At his home, Ramu eagerly listened to the stories shared by his father's returning followers. Tales of Rajini electrifying rallies of hundreds of thousands with his fearless calls for resistance against Imperial tyranny.

"Your father is a lion among men!" they would say.

"There is no equal to him in all of country!"

From the pride in their voices, the young boy understood just how beloved and revered his Baba was to the common people. They saw him as the living embodiment of the struggle's spirit.

But Ramu also sensed his mother's growing anxiety.

Parvathi pleaded constantly with Rajini to slow down before his health failed or the British authorities finally execute him.

"How long can you keep fighting this rising tide?" she asked desperately. "Shouldn't we just accept what little mercies the British concede?"

Rajini caressed her cheek gently. "You speak out of love and worry for this family. But I fight for something beyond ourselves - for the freedom and dignity of generations past, present, and future. That is a sacred trust I cannot abandon."

Seeing that further argument was fruitless, Parvathi simply embraced her husband, before their next trip to Delhi where he is establishing an ashram. She realized that Rajini no longer belonged just to her - he was now leader of a people's struggle sweeping all of India toward emancipation.

Rajini cherished the moments when he sat down with his son, Ramu, to impart timeless wisdom through stories and fables. These father-son sessions were more than mere storytelling; they were precious opportunities for Rajini to instill invaluable life lessons and moral teachings in Ramu's young mind.

As the evening sun painted hues of gold across the horizon, Rajini and Ramu would often retreat to a quiet corner of their home. The air would be filled with a sense of warmth and anticipation as Rajini, with a gentle smile, would beckon Ramu to join him.

Seated under the spreading branches of an ancient banyan tree or by the crackling fireplace on colder evenings, Rajini would begin weaving tales that transported young Ramu into a world of wonder and wisdom.

The Wise Sage and the Kind Prince: Rajini narrated tales of a wise sage who, through his profound teachings, guided a young prince on the path of righteousness and compassion. These stories were filled with anecdotes about courage, integrity, and the importance of empathy.

Along with stories from The Ramayana, The Mahabharatha, Rajini narrated the stories of western world also.

The Fable of the Ant and the Grasshopper: Through relatable fables like this, Rajini taught Ramu the virtues of diligence and foresight. He emphasized the value of hard work and preparation, drawing parallels to life's challenges and the importance of being prepared for the future.

The Story of the Tree of Unity: Rajini spun imaginative stories about a tree that flourished because each of its branches, representing different communities and beliefs, worked together in harmony. Through this, he conveyed the significance of unity, tolerance, and mutual respect among diverse individuals.

Tales of Courage and Sacrifice: Rajini recounted stories of heroes who displayed unwavering courage and selflessness in the face of adversity. These narratives aimed to inspire Ramu and impart the essence of resilience, bravery, and standing up for what is right.

With each story, Rajini wove a web of life lessons, subtly embedding moral values and ethical principles. His storytelling wasn't solely for entertainment; it was a vessel for imparting age-old wisdom, nurturing Ramu's character, and guiding him to become a compassionate and principled individual.

Ramu listened intently, his young eyes wide with wonder and curiosity. He absorbed his father's teachings eagerly, his imagination ignited by the vivid imagery of Rajini's narratives. Through these stories, Rajini not only shared his wisdom but also strengthened the bond between father and son, creating cherished memories that would last a lifetime.

These moments of storytelling weren't just about passing time; they were precious instances where Rajini, as a loving father, sculpted the foundation of Ramu's moral compass, nurturing him into a person of integrity, empathy, and resilience.

Chapter 28
Rowlatt Act & Plan to Go Beyond

Rajini called for a meeting and expressed his views to send Varada chary, Yadagiri and some others to other villages and nearby states for the enhancement of freedom movement. They all bid good bye to Rajini and left to the designated places with teary eyes. From all these years they were fighting shoulder to shoulder, but now new leadership is required in many areas. Rajini being aa true leader has made and trained a pack of infallible leaders. He led them with example.

Rowlatt Act

That year, the independence movement faced a major test of strength and unity. The British unveiled the exploitative Rowlatt Act, which essentially continued the oppression of martial law even after the First World War had ended.

The Anarchical and Revolutionary Crimes Act of 1919, popularly known as the Rowlatt Act, was a law, applied during the British India period. It was a legislative council act passed by the Imperial Legislative Council in Delhi on 18 March 1919, indefinitely extending the emergency measures of preventive indefinite detention, imprisonment without trial and judicial review enacted in the

Defence of India Act 1915 during the First World War. It was enacted in the light of a perceived threat from revolutionary nationalists of re-engaging in similar conspiracies as had occurred during the war

which the Government felt the lapse of the Defence of India Act would enable.

Purpose

The British Colonial Government passed the "Rowlatt Act" which gave power to the police to arrest any person without any reason. The purpose of the Act was to curb the growing nationalist upsurge in the country.

Passed on the recommendations of the Rowlatt Committee and named after its president, Sir Sidney Rowlatt, the act effectively authorized the colonial British government to imprison any person suspected of terrorism living in British India for up to two years, and gave the colonial authorities power to deal with all revolutionary activities.

The unpopular legislation provided for stricter control of the press arrests without warrant, indefinite detention without trial, and juryless in camera trials for proscribed political acts The accused were denied the right to know the accusers and the evidence used in the trial. Those convicted were required to deposit securities upon release, and were prohibited from taking part in any political, educational, or religious activities. On the report of the committee, headed by Justice Rowlatt, two bills were introduced in the Central

Legislature on 6 February 1919. These bills came to be known as "Black Bills". They gave enormous powers to the police to search a place and arrest any person they disapproved of without warrant. Despite much opposition, the Rowlatt Act was passed on 18 March 1919. The purpose of the act was to curb the growing nationalist upsurge in the country. Under the Rowlatt act 1919, the chief justice was empowered to decide on the immediate custody of the accused between the trial and release on bail for smooth implementation of the act. The act also provides a penalty for disobedience of any order promulgated under sections 22 and 27 of the act, which is imprisonment for a maximum of six months or a fine of Rs. 500 or both.

Effect

Madan Mohan Malaviya resigned from the Imperial legislative council in protest against the act. The act also infuriated many other Indian leaders and the public, which caused the government to implement repressive measures. Gandhi and others thought that constitutional opposition to the measure was fruitless, so on 6 April, a hartal took place. This was an event in which Indians suspended businesses and went on strikes and would fast, pray and hold public meetings against the 'Black Act' as a sign of their opposition and civil disobedience would be offered against the law.

The Rowlatt Act came into effect on 21 March 1919. In Punjab the protest movement was very strong, and on 10 April two leaders of the congress, Dr. Satyapal and Saifuddin Kitchlew, were arrested and taken secretly to Dharamsala.

Rajini blasted the unjust law before massive crowds across the country. In his area, he called for nonviolent civil disobedience until it was repealed. People responded to his appeal, downing tools in factories, boycotting British goods, and marching peacefully in defiance.

Faced with disciplined nationwide resistance, the rattled British were forced to revoke the hated Rowlatt Act within weeks. It was an emphatic victory that proved the potency of mass strategic nonviolence. For Rajini, this was confirmation that a previously slumbering people had awoken and found their voice at last.

Why revoke???

If the Rowlatt Act had been fully implemented in India in 1919, it would have had significant and far-reaching consequences on the Indian freedom struggle and the political landscape of the country.

The Rowlatt Act was a repressive legislation introduced by the British colonial government to curb political dissent and suppress Indian nationalist movements.

Some of the potential outcomes and consequences of the full implementation of the Rowlatt Act in 1919:

Mass Protests and Civil Disobedience: The Rowlatt Act would likely have faced strong opposition from the Indian population. It would have led to widespread protests, demonstrations, and civil disobedience campaigns against the oppressive measures. This could have united Indians across different regions, religions, and backgrounds against British rule.

Massacres, mass arrests and Public Outrage: The implementation of the Rowlatt Act could have escalated tensions and resulted in more massacres, British troops killing hundreds of unarmed Indian civilians. This event would have intensified public

anger and mobilized more Indians against British rule.

Expansion of Nationalist Movements: The harsh measures of the Rowlatt Act could have radicalized moderate leaders and organizations, pushing them to adopt more radical and militant approaches in their struggle for independence. This might have accelerated the growth and influence of the Indian National Congress and other nationalist groups.

Emergence of New Leaders: The repressive nature of the Rowlatt Act could have led to the emergence of new leaders who were more radical and willing to take direct action against British rule. Leaders like Mahatma Gandhi, who advocated nonviolent resistance, might have gained prominence even earlier due to their ability to unify and mobilize people against the Act.

International Attention: The implementation of such a draconian law could have attracted international attention and condemnation, possibly increasing pressure on the British government to reconsider its colonial policies in India.

Economic Impact: Widespread protests and civil unrest could have disrupted normal life and economic activities, potentially leading to economic losses for the British colonial administration and their local collaborators.

Escalation of Violence: The implementation of the Rowlatt Act might have pushed some factions within the Indian population to resort to violence and terrorism as a means of resistance, leading to an escalation of conflicts between the British authorities and Indian nationalists.

Stronger Unity: The Act could have acted as a catalyst for unifying different factions of the Indian society against a common enemy – British colonial rule. This unity could have paved the way for a more coordinated and potent resistance movement.

Accelerated Independence Movement: The severe repression under the Rowlatt Act might have accelerated the process of India's struggle for independence, as it would have further exposed the unjust and autocratic nature of British rule to a wider Indian audience.

The full implementation of the Rowlatt Act in 1919 would likely have intensified the Indian freedom struggle, leading to increased opposition, mobilization, and a potentially faster trajectory towards eventual independence.

The British understood that it does a lot harm to them than good, and then revoked the act amidst Civil Disobidience.

That evening, Rajini returned home weary but elated. "What was accomplished today will echo through history," he told Parvathi. "India has discovered her true strength through unity. A mighty movement has been born that will soon deliver our freedom."

Parvathi smiled, allowing herself to believe that happier times may indeed be dawning for future generations. Outside, hope and fervor pulsed through the land like an electric current. The diverse peoples of India were forging bonds that would shake the mighty British Raj to its very core.

Chapter 29
The Battle Intensifies

Emboldened by victory against the Rowlatt Act, the independence movement gained unstoppable momentum under Rajini's leadership.

At last, freedom from colonial oppression seemed imminent. But the British had no intention of relinquishing control over the Crown Jewel of its Empire. Despite growing unrest, the Viceroy ordered draconian measures to crush civil disobedience across India. Protestors were shot dead in the Punjab. In Amritsar, hundreds of peaceful demonstrators were massacred at Jallianwala Bagh.

Rajini was horrified and enraged by the callous brutality. He realized the nonviolent movement now faced its greatest trial yet. If people turned to vengeance, all hope of independence through principled civil disobedience would be lost. So Rajini doubled down on discipline and unity, touring the country to calm angry crowds baying for British blood.

"Our protest must remain peaceful for freedom to prevail." But privately, Rajini seethed that the British continued to repress the legitimate aspirations of millions with violent terror. "How long can I convince our people to absorb blow after blow without retaliating?" he asked Parvathi worriedly.

She saw the toll this long freedom struggle had taken on her beloved husband, aging him beyond his years. "You have accomplished the seemingly impossible by awakening our nation," she said. "No man could have given more. Please, for our family's sake, leave matters in the next generation's hands now."

Rajini shook his head resolutely. "I cannot rest while our people continue suffering oppression. But your counsel is wise - we must groom new leaders to carry forth our ideals." So Rajini actively mentored emerging stalwarts like Ahmed and Patel, instilling in them the ideologies and strategies underpinning the independence movement. They in turn idolized Rajini, knowing his towering legacy would pass on through them.

He established an Ashram in a nearby half ruined temple and started training the satyagrahis to fight the biggest battle yet to come. Ahmed and Patel took very important tasks of arranging protests and strikes against the British, while Rajini looked after training, grooming and motivation.

A Ruby from Jallian Wala Bagh

The acrid smell of smoke filled Lakshman's nostrils as he stumbled through the streets of Amritsar. All around him lay the ruins of the place reduced to rubble, corpses strewn amid the wreckage. An eerie silence hung in the air, the only sounds being his labored breathing and the crackling of fires still burning.

It was as if some terrible storm had swept through the holy city, leaving utter devastation in its wake. But Lakshman knew the truth—there had been no natural disaster, only man's inhumanity to man.

The events of the previous day played on an endless loop in his mind. He had been at the Jallian walla Bagh with his family. Without warning, the British troops had blocked all exits and opened fire indiscriminately on the unarmed crowd.

The Massacre:

Amritsar, a city in the Punjab region of India, was under martial law, and a British officer, Brigadier General Reginald Dyer, was in charge.

As part of the protest against the Rowlatt Act (a law that allowed for indefinite detention without trial), a large crowd, including men, women, and children, had gathered at Jallianwala Bagh, a public garden in Amritsar, to peacefully protest and listen to speeches. Unaware of the proclamation that banned public gatherings, a peaceful crowd of around 10,000 to 20,000 people had assembled in the enclosed Jallianwala Bagh.

Without any warning, General Dyer and a group of soldiers arrived at the garden. He ordered his troops to block the only exit, then opened fire on the unarmed and unsuspecting crowd. The soldiers, positioned at the entrance, started shooting indiscriminately into the crowd for about 10-15 minutes, aiming at the densest sections of people.

People tried to escape, some climbing the walls, but the exit was blocked, leading to chaos and a stampede. Many were killed by the bullets, while others were crushed in the stampede or drowned while trying to escape by jumping into a well inside the garden.

Lakshman, a teenager, remembered the panic, the screams, as people scrambled in vain to escape the onslaught of bullets. His mother had pushed him to the ground, shielding him with her body as the shots rang out. When the firing finally ceased, an eerie silence fell upon the blood-soaked gardens.

That was when Lakshman realized with horror—his mother and father lay lifeless beside him, their eyes open and unseeing. All around lay the bodies of brothers, sisters, friends—cut down in their prime. The once vibrant Bagh was now a charnel house, strewn with hundreds of corpses. The actual number of casualties is disputed. Official estimates by the British at the time were around 379 killed and over 1,200 wounded, but other sources, including Indian nationalists, claimed the numbers were much higher, possibly over a thousand deaths.

Somehow, Lakshman had managed to crawl out, unscathed but utterly broken inside. Now, as he walked through the ruins of Amritsar, the full magnitude of the tragedy hit him. His entire family, his entire world, had been wiped out in a single day by the ruthless British.

He had no idea what to do or where to go. As the eldest son, it was now his duty to take care of his younger siblings. But they too were gone, their childhoods and futures stolen away. Lakshman was utterly alone in the world for the first time. An all-consuming emptiness gripped his heart where once there had been love and laughter.

Stumbling through a narrow alley, he spotted a small temple untouched by the violence. Seeking solace, he entered and collapsed before the idol of Shiva, tears streaming down his face. "Why?" he cried out in anguish. "Why did you let this happen, Mahadev? Where were you when we needed you most?"

There was no answer from the silent deity. Lakshman knew the gods could not intervene in human affairs, but he had always taken comfort in their benevolent presence. Now even his faith lay in tatters, unable to comprehend the senseless carnage of the past day.

As he wept, a gentle hand rested on his shoulder. Lakshman looked up to see an elderly priest gazing down at him with kind eyes. "There there, child. Let it all out," he said softly. When Lakshman had calmed somewhat, the priest sat beside him. "I know your pain all too well, beta. This is a day that will forever haunt our city. But we must not lose hope—hatred and vengeance will only breed more suffering."

"How can you say that, pandit-ji?" Lakshman cried angrily. "Those butchers killed everyone I loved without mercy! They deserve to be punished!"

The priest nodded sadly. "An eye for an eye makes the whole world blind, Lakshman. Violence will not undo this violence or bring your family back. That is the path of the oppressor, not the oppressed."

"Then what is to be done?" Lakshman asked, his voice hollow with despair. "How do we survive this ruin?"

"We survive through our spirit, which can never be broken no matter what the body endures," the priest replied. "And we honor the martyrs of today by continuing their fight for justice through non-violent, lawful means. Hatred must be fought with love."

His words kindled a small flame of hope in Lakshman's heart, even as anger and grief still raged within. "You speak wisdom, pandit-ji. But how can one small boy make any difference?"

The priest smiled. "You'd be surprised what one determined soul can achieve. There are others working to end the British Raj and give our country its rightful independence through peaceful resistance. Seek them out—that is the path forward from this tragedy."

Lakshman took a deep breath, squaring his shoulders with newfound resolve. "Then that is what I will do. I will join the fight and make the killers pay...not through violence but by seeing to it that India is free at last. It's what my family would have wanted." The priest nodded, pleased. "That is the spirit.

Now go in peace, beta, and know that you do not walk this path alone."

Rising unsteadily to his feet, Lakshman took one last look around the ruined temple that had given him solace. Then, with purpose in his step, he walked out into the ashes of Amritsar and whatever future awaited. The fire of vengeance in his heart had been quenched, but in its place now burned a fiery determination to honor his loved ones' memory through nonviolent revolution. His journey was just beginning.

Chapter 30
Call of Action

Lakshman walked for days after leaving Amritsar, putting as much distance as possible between himself and the site of the massacre. All around him, the scars of British rule were evident - from the poverty-stricken villages to the looming presence of colonial infrastructure.

As he passed through small towns along the Grand Trunk Road, whispers of the Jallianwala Bagh tragedy preceded him. People looked at him with pity, yet also a newfound respect as a survivor of that dark day. Some offered him food and shelter out of kindness.

Despite their own struggles, these everyday Indians gave Lakshman hope. Their resilience in the face of oppression reminded him of the priest's words - that the spirit of a nation could never truly be broken. If these nameless people could carry on with their lives, then so too must he continue his journey.

One evening, as Lakshman rested in a village, an old man approached. "You're the boy from Amritsar, aren't you?" he asked. When Lakshman nodded, the man said "Come with me, beta. There are others who've been waiting to meet you."Piqued by the mysterious statement, Lakshman followed the man to a secluded hut. Inside sat four young men, conversing in hushed tones around an oil lamp. They fell silent as Lakshman entered, regarding him intently.

The old man spoke. "These brave sons risk their lives every day to oppose the British through non-violent civil disobedience. Word of your ordeal has spread, Lakshman - and they believe you can help the cause."

One of the men stepped forward. "My name is Bhagawan Singh. We could use someone with your experience to spread awareness of our movement. The British want us to forget what happened at Jallianwala Bagh. But the whole country must know of their brutality so that independence is inevitable."

Lakshman was taken aback by the impassioned words. These were no ordinary villagers - they possessed a fiery zeal to rid India of its colonial shackles through peaceful resistance.

"I have nothing left to lose," Lakshman replied. "Tell me what you need of me and it shall be done. But I seek to join a larger struggle - is there a leader coordinating resistance across the nation?"

Bhagawan Singh smiled. "There is indeed - the one man truly uniting our fight. His name is Rajini Kantha Reddy, and now he is in Delhi. From his base in Delhi he is building an army of satyagrahis to challenge British rule through non-cooperation."

Hearing this, Lakshman's heart soared with renewed purpose.

At last, he had a direction - to reach the capital and pledge himself to this Rajini Kantha's cause. "Then to Delhi is where I must go. Will you help me spread word of the massacre to rally more to our side?"

"It would be our honor," Bhagawan Singh replied. And so began Lakshman's work with the resistance movement, sharing his tragic tale across towns and villages to awaken the fire of rebellion in ordinary Indians' hearts. Through civil disobedience and non-cooperation, they sought to make the nation ungovernable for the British through peaceful means.

Weeks passed as Lakshman spread word of the atrocity with Bhagawan Singh and the others. The movement gained momentum, with support swelling wherever the tragic story was shared. Soon, it was time for Lakshman's long-awaited journey to continue alone.

The parting from his new comrades was bittersweet. "We could not have come so far without you, brother," Bhagawan Singh said, embracing him. "But greater work awaits in Delhi. Go now and pledge yourself to Rajini - he is fighting at a massive scale to fulfill the Indian dream of swaraj."

With their blessings, Lakshman resumed his northward travel along roads thronged with fellow pilgrims. As he walked, the signs of oppression seemed to intensify the closer he drew to the imperial capital. British soldiers stood on every street corner, keeping a watchful eye for dissent.

One afternoon, Lakshman witnessed an incident that tested his commitment to non-violence. A group of soldiers were mercilessly beating an elderly farmer who had dared to question their authority. Rage and vengeance welled up inside the young man, begging to be unleashed.

He clenched his fists, tempted to intervene by any means necessary. But the priest's words echoed in his mind - violence would only beget more violence, and go against everything the resistance movement stood for. With immense willpower, Lakshman forced himself to look away and continue on his path.

That night as he rested, doubts crept in. Was non-violence truly the answer in the face of such brutality? Or were more forceful measures needed to end colonial rule once and for all? The conflict between his desire for justice and adherence to satyagraha principles left Lakshman feeling torn.

It was during this dark hour of uncertainty that a chance encounter lifted his spirits once more. In a small roadside temple, Lakshman spotted an elderly man deep in prayer, radiating an aura of profound calm. Something about his presence put Lakshman's turbulent mind at ease.

As if sensing his turmoil, the man spoke without turning. "Doubts will come to all who walk the path of ahimsa, young one. But within you lies the strength to overcome them through love and truth alone."

Lakshman was stunned. It was as if this stranger could peer into his very soul.

When the man finally faced him, Lakshman gasped - in his kindly eyes shone the same fire of conviction he had seen in Rajini Kantha from descriptions of Bhagawan Singh. This could only be the man himself.

Bowing low, Lakshman said "Forgive me, sir. I am Lakshman, a survivor of Jallianwala Bagh come to offer my services to your cause. But tell me - how can non-violence truly defeat an empire built on violence?"

Rajini Kantha smiled, placing a hand on Lakshman's shoulder. "Come, and I shall show you the power of ahimsa through our work. There, all your doubts will vanish - for love is the only force capable of dissolving even the hardest of hearts. Your thirstful journey is over, Lakshman. It is not only my cause, it is our cause, the nation's cause. You are home at last. He introduced Lakshman to Parvathi and Ramu. "

Journey to the Rebellion

The next morning, Lakshman awoke feeling more at peace than he had in months. After a simple breakfast with Rajini Kantha in the temple courtyard, the revolutionary leader gave him a tour of the sprawling complex that served as headquarters for the resistance movement.

"This is where thousands of satyagrahis from across the country receive training in the principles of non-violent civil disobedience," Rajini Kantha explained. "We teach them how to confront tyranny through courage, discipline and love alone."

As they walked the grounds, Lakshman saw groups of men and women practicing techniques of peaceful protest - from courting arrest through strategic disobedience to enduring police brutality without retaliation.

Their discipline and commitment was inspiring to behold.

Rajini Kantha then led him to an open-air training arena. "Here is where you will begin your new life's work, Lakshman. Are you ready to dedicate yourself fully to the cause of Indian independence through ahimsa?"

Lakshman knelt before the leader, head bowed. "With all my heart, I pledge myself to you and this movement, guruji. Teach me how I may best serve to honor the martyrs of Amritsar."

Rajini Kantha smiled, placing a hand on Lakshman's head in blessing. "Rise then, and let your training commence."

Over the next few months, Lakshman not only became the family of Rajini but also immersed himself in the rigorous satyagraha regimen under Rajini Kantha's watchful eye. He practiced withstanding police assaults without fighting back, even as anger and vengeance still simmered within.

Through meditation and philosophical discussions, Rajini Kantha helped Lakshman understand the futility of violence as a means of social change. "Hatred cannot drive out hatred - only love can do that," the leader often said.

Gradually, as the flames of his rage cooled, Lakshman began to see the inherent strength in meeting oppression with courage, discipline and soul force alone. Non-violence, he realized, was the most powerful weapon of all for dismantling an empire of violence from within. As his skills improved, Lakshman assisted in training new recruits.

One day, a young woman named Asha joined their cohort. Though shy at first, her determination shone through. During sparring practice (for self defence), Lakshman went easy on Asha out of chivalry. But she surprised him with her ferocity, knocking him to the ground in a deft maneuver. Grinning, she offered her hand. "Never underestimate a woman, Comrade."

From that day, a bond of friendship and respect formed between them. Asha proved as dedicated to the cause as any man, and soon became Lakshman's closest confidante within the movement. For Parvathi, Asha was like Lakshmi - their lost daughter.

Chapter 31
Mentoring

In the serene ambiance of their home, Rajini found moments to introduce Ramu to the principles of Marx and communism, using captivating analogies and relatable case studies. Seated comfortably in a cozy room adorned with books and artifacts, Rajini began weaving a tapestry of ideas and ideals that aimed to explain the essence of Marx's philosophy in a way that a young mind could comprehend.

The Analogy of Sharing Toys: Rajini initiated the discussion by comparing the act of sharing toys among friends to the concept of communal ownership advocated by Marx. He illustrated how, just like friends sharing toys to play together happily, communism envisioned a society where resources were shared equally among everyone, fostering cooperation and eliminating disparities.

The Story of a Village Farm: Drawing from real-life examples, Rajini narrated a tale of a village farm where each farmer contributed their labor equally, and the produce was distributed fairly among all the families. This anecdote illustrated the principles of collective effort, fairness, and the elimination of class distinctions.

In a tranquil village nestled amidst rolling hills and lush greenery, there existed a farm that stood as a testament to the principles of cooperation and equality. This farm, owned collectively by the villagers, was a living embodiment of the ideals Rajini aimed to impart to young Ramu regarding Marx's principles.

The village farm was a picturesque landscape where rows of crops flourished under the golden sunlight. Each family in the village contributed their labor, time, and knowledge to nurture the land, fostering a sense of unity and shared responsibility.

Rajini vividly narrated to Ramu the tale of this harmonious farming community, where every villager, regardless of their background or status, had an equal say in decision-making and shared ownership of the farm's produce.

Throughout the agricultural seasons, from the sowing of seeds to the harvesting of crops, the villagers worked hand in hand. They toiled together, tending to the fields with care and dedication, ensuring the well-being of the farm and the bounty it would yield.

The principle of collective ownership and equitable distribution was at the heart of this farm. When the time for harvesting arrived, the fruits of their labor were shared fairly among all the families in the village. Every household received an equal share of the produce, ensuring that no family went without sustenance.

This farm was not just about cultivating crops; it was a testament to the community's solidarity and commitment to each other's welfare. The villagers understood that their collective efforts were essential for the farm's success, and they rejoiced together in the abundance it provided.

Through this story, Rajini conveyed to Ramu the essence of Marx's vision – a society where resources were shared equitably, labor was valued equally, and the benefits of collective efforts were enjoyed by all. The village farm exemplified the ideals of cooperation, fairness, and unity that Rajini wished to instill in his son's understanding of a just and harmonious society.

As Rajini painted this vivid picture of the village farm, Ramu absorbed the profound lessons embedded within the narrative, learning not just about farming practices but also about the importance of collective effort, sharing, and the values of communism and equality.

Ramu's eyes sparkled with curiosity as his father described the harmonious workings of the village farm. He envisioned the rows of flourishing crops, the diligent farmers, and the sense of unity that permeated the community. Rajini's vivid storytelling painted a vibrant picture that stirred Ramu's imagination.

Upon the tale's conclusion, Ramu, brimming with wonder and intrigue, began to ponder the intricacies of the farm's collective ownership model. With innocence and enthusiasm, he posed insightful questions that reflected his eagerness to comprehend the deeper nuances of the story.

"Father," Ramu began, his voice laced with curiosity, "how did everyone in the village agree on how to share the produce? What if someone wanted more than others?"

Rajini, heartened by Ramu's thoughtful inquiry, warmly embraced the opportunity to delve into the intricacies of equitable distribution and cooperative living.

"Ah, my dear Ramu," Rajini replied, a sense of pride in his son's inquisitiveness, "that's an astute question. In the village farm, decisions were made together through discussions and consensus. The villagers believed in sharing the produce equally among all families, ensuring fairness and unity."

Ramu, contemplating his father's words, continued, "But what if someone didn't want to work as hard as the others? Would that be fair to everyone else?"

Rajini, impressed by Ramu's insightful query, explained further, "In a community where everyone shares ownership, it's important that each person contributes their fair share of effort. Cooperation and mutual support were the foundations of the farm's success. They believed that by working together, everyone benefits equally."

Ramu's thirst for understanding and quest for knowledge propelled the conversation further. His father, gratified by Ramu's curiosity, used these moments to instill valuable lessons about cooperation, fairness, and the importance of collective effort in achieving communal prosperity.

Meanwhile, news of the resistance was spreading across the country. Every day, more Indians arrived at the temple seeking to pledge themselves to Rajini Kantha's leadership. His message of non-violent defiance was inspiring a nationwide revolution.

One evening, as Lakshman relaxed with Asha after training, Rajini Kantha summoned them. "The time has come for your first mission, my children," he said gravely. "The British are planning a major crackdown. We must spread word to all our cells to prepare for civil disobedience on an unprecedented scale."

Lakshman and Asha listened intently as Rajini Kantha outlined their covert operation. Under cover of night, they were to travel across northern India delivering encrypted messages and coordinating resistance activities. It was a high-risk mission, but one that could turn the tide in their struggle.

"I know I can depend on you both to carry out this vital work," Rajini Kantha said. "Go now with my blessings, and may truth and non-violence guide your path."

That night, as Lakshman and Asha made preparations under the light of the moon, he turned to his friend. "I never thought

I'd find purpose again after Amritsar. But because of guruji and this movement, I feel whole for the first time."

Asha squeezed his hand. "We've both known great loss, Comrade.

But through satyagraha, we can honor the martyrs and build the

India of their dreams. Are you ready for what lies ahead?"

Lakshman nodded, squaring his shoulders. "I was born ready. For freedom!"

And with that cry, the two young revolutionaries slipped into the night to begin their dangerous mission. As they rode off into the darkness, Lakshman felt only courage and resolve in his heart - for he now understood the power of non-violence to overcome any obstacle and change the course of history. The real work was only just beginning.

Gathering Support

Over the next few months, Lakshman and Asha traveled tirelessly across northern India, evading British patrols under the cloak of night. By day, they hid in forests and remote villages, coordinating resistance activities with underground satyagrahi cells.

It was grueling work, but seeing the passion of ordinary Indians reignited Lakshman's spirit. In every town, supporters swelled the ranks of those committed to non-cooperation. Through peaceful marches, strikes and other acts of civil disobedience, the movement was gaining unprecedented momentum.

One evening, as the two sat resting after a long day, Lakshman turned to Asha. Do you ever wonder what might have been, had the massacre not happened? Would I still be a farmer's son in Amritsar, oblivious to the greater struggle?

Asha smiled softly. Perhaps this was all meant to be, Comrade. Your family sacrificed so that through you, thousands more may be awakened to the cause of freedom. We must honor their memory by continuing the fight.

Lakshman nodded, taking comfort in her words. You're right, as always. Come, there is still work to be done this night!

And so their journey continued. Over time, Lakshman and Asha developed an easy camaraderie, finding solace in each other's company on the lonely roads. Their bond grew deeper with every peril they faced and overcame through courage and faith in their principles.

One night, as they rested in a village, Lakshman was roused by shouts. Rushing out, he saw a group of drunk British soldiers accosting the womenfolk. Without thinking, he raced forward and shoved the men away from their intended victims.

The soldiers rounded on Lakshman, enraged. You'll pay for that, boy! one slurred, drawing his knife. But before they could attack, the entire village surrounded the revolutionaries, shouting slogans of defiance. Outnumbered, the soldiers backed away, hurling threats as they departed.

Turning to the villagers, Lakshman said calmly, We must stand up to such injustices through lawful and peaceful means alone. Violence will only beget more violence. Who among you will join our movement to end colonial rule through satyagraha?

To his delight, every man, woman and child in the village volunteered then and there. That night, as Lakshman and Asha continued on, a new fire of determination burned within him. The people were truly becoming the force that could shake the very foundations of the Raj.

A few weeks later, as winter set in, Lakshman fell ill with fever in a remote forest hideout. Asha tended to him with herbal remedies and prayers, refusing to leave his side. For three long days, his life hung in the balance.

On the fourth morning, Lakshman awoke to find Asha asleep, her head resting on his arm in exhaustion. As he gazed upon her face, serene in repose, he was struck by her inner beauty and the depth of care she had shown him. A strange new feeling stirred in his heart. Shaking off such thoughts, Lakshman gently woke Asha. Thank you for saving my life, he said hoarsely. I don't know what I'd do without you.

Asha smiled, relief flooding her eyes. You had me worried there for a while, Comrade! Now come, we have a revolution to win.

Refreshed and reinvigorated, Lakshman and Asha resumed their work.

Over the coming months, the movement grew from a few scattered cells into a nationwide phenomenon. Wherever the two traveled, people rallied to their call, swelling the ranks of non-cooperators.

One night, as winter gave way to spring, Lakshman and Asha stopped in a village for rest. To their surprise, they were greeted as honored guests by the villagers. News of their exploits had spread far and wide.

We are with you in spirit and solidarity, the headman said, presenting them with gifts of food, clothing and money for their cause. Though we cannot join you physically, know that this entire village supports your mission. You have given us hope!

Overcome with emotion, Lakshman embraced the man. Thank you for your kindness, Comrade. Because of people like you, our dream of swaraj is coming closer each day. The British may rule us for now, but in our hearts we are already free!

His words were met with loud cheers. That night, as Lakshman gazed at the stars, he felt a surge of pride at how far they had come. Through courage and faith in their principles, he and Asha were igniting a revolution that could no longer be stopped.

The end of British rule was coming - he could feel it in his soul.,

Chapter 32
Plans for Uprising

Spring turned to summer as Lakshman and Asha's efforts bore fruit across the nation. Where once there had been a few scattered cells, now every town and village echoed with slogans of defiance against the Raj.

Ordinary Indians from all walks of life were joining the satyagraha movement in unprecedented numbers. Peasants left their fields until land taxes were reduced, students boycotted classes, workers abandoned their factories and mills.

Through non-violent mass protests and non-cooperation, the resistance was crippling the British war machine from within. Yet the colonial government responded with increasing brutality, banning public meetings and arresting thousands of activists.

It was clear more drastic action was needed to force the empire's hand. And so, one sultry night, Lakshman and Asha received new orders from Rajini Kantha - to return to Delhi at once, for a top-secret mission of vital importance.

Upon arriving at the temple headquarters, they were ushered into the Guruji's private chambers. My children, the time has come to deliver the final blow that can shake the British to their core, Rajini Kantha said gravely.

We will launch the largest satyagraha campaign yet across the entire subcontinent. Every city, town and village will rise up through mass civil disobedience. When the people's will is shown in such force, the Raj will have no choice but to concede to our demands for swaraj.

Lakshman and Asha listened, hearts swelling with pride and anticipation. But what role have you for us, guruji? Lakshman asked eagerly.

Rajini Kantha smiled. I knew you would not wish to sit this out. Very well - you two will lead covert operations to coordinate resistance activities across the major cities. It is an immensely risky mission, but one that could determine the uprising's success. Are you ready?

Without hesitation, both revolutionaries knelt before their leader. We have lived our lives for this moment, Guruji.

Command us as you see fit - we shall not fail.

Rajini Kantha placed his hands in blessing. Then go with my blessings, and may truth be your shield. Depart under cover of darkness. The time to shake the foundations of empire is upon us!

That very night, as a crescent moon rose over Delhi, Lakshman and Asha slipped away into the shadows once more. Over the coming weeks, they traveled from city to city under assumed identities, meeting underground cells and finalizing plans.

Love in the Time of Revolution

In Calcutta, Bombay, Madras - everywhere the fire of rebellion burned bright. On the appointed day, thousands would lay siege to government buildings through mass civil disobedience until independence was won.

As the fated day drew closer, Lakshman and Asha doubled their efforts. Yet amidst it all, Lakshman found himself increasingly drawn to his friend. Her courage, compassion and beauty moved him like none other.

One evening, as they rested by a campfire, Lakshman gathered his courage. Asha, ever since we met you've been my closest companion. But I feel there is more between us than just friendship. Will you -

Before he could finish, Asha placed a finger to his lips. Hush now, Comrade. Our duty to the movement comes first, as does the dream we fight for. When India is free, then we shall see what the future holds. For now, let this be enough.

Lakshman nodded, heart swelling with love and gratitude for her understanding. You're right, as always. Come, our work is not yet done!

And so they plunged back into preparations, putting all else aside for the uprising's success. At last, the fated day arrived when the entire nation would rise as one in peaceful revolution. After so much struggle and sacrifice, the final battle was about to begin.

The British authorities grew wary of Rajini's undiminished influence. They attempted to isolate him by portraying him as a militant fringe element undermining serious nationalist dialogue. British propaganda suggested his radical activism actually jeopardized the moderate progress being made through official channels.

But the people knew Rajini as the heart and soul of the freedom struggle. And they continued rallying to his call, inspired by his willingness to sacrifice his all for their emancipation.

"How is it that the spirit of this stubborn man remains unbroken despite all our efforts?" the frustrated Viceroy questioned his intelligence chief. "Why does he still command such authority and adulation?"

The chief narrowed his eyes. **"Because Sir, ideas are bulletproof. And as long as Rajini lives, his ideals fuel hope of independence in millions. His legend is now beyond any man's power to extinguish."**

The Viceroy slammed his fist on the desk angrily. "Then we shall see this rebel's resolve tested to its limits!"

In the following months, Rajini's nonviolent protests were met with ever harsher crackdowns. Key supporters were arrested on sedition charges. Public gatherings he addressed were broken up violently. But the undeterred crusader pressed on heedless of personal cost or danger.

Lakshman, Asha and fifty other satyagrahis were killed in the huge crush. An insider poisoned the food for the British money and immunity. The insider happened to be Ambarish - a close aide of Lakshman during all his travels. The British shot and killed Ambarish, when he went to collect his bounty.

This has devastated Rajini, Parvathi and Ramu. Parvathi kept crying the same way she did for Lakshmi. Rajini just fell silent and started looking into the Abyss, thinking that he is guilty and the blood is on his hands. Ramu was clenching fists with anger, if got a chance, he wants to shoot all the British at once. But as the British official said, they have tested the emotional resolute of the mammoth Rajini.

The mammoth fell down, but it was temporary. For India's freedom he lived, for her masses he fought and if need be, for her future he would die without remorse. This single-minded sense of purpose sustained Rajini through every tribulation inflicted upon him and his movement.

Chapter 33
Missing

One evening after returning home bloodied from a protest, Rajini was alarmed to find Ramu missing.

"Some British officers dragged him away this morning, accusing him of aiding your antigovernment activities," a servant informed worriedly. "We know not where they took him!"

Rajini immediately raced to the local British administrator's office, roaring: "That boy has nothing to do with politics! Tell me where you are holding my innocent son or else!"

The cold-eyed administrator leaned forward. "Consider this a warning, Mr Reddy. Restrain your agitations, or the next time it will not be just your son but your entire treasonous family we imprison."

Rajini trembled with fury at this threat. But he realized he could not allow the British to use his loved ones as leverage over him. If it came to the ultimate test, he was prepared to sacrifice even their safety to continue guiding India towards freedom.

Rajini returned home exhausted after securing Ramu's release from British custody. Though rattled, the spirited boy was more awed than fearful of the experience. But a distraught Parvathi clasped her son tight, glaring accusingly at Rajini. She could not get out of the grief of Lakshman and Asha, and now the bomb of Ramu's disappearance is too hard for any mother to stay calm and cool minded.

"How could you let our only son be threatened this way?" she cried. "Does your devotion to this confounded movement eclipse even your family?"

Rajini reached out conciliatorily, but Parvathi recoiled from his touch. "Enough is enough!" she snapped, before storming off.

That night, Rajini found Parvathi weeping silently by Lakshmi's caricature. He sat down gently beside her.

"My loyal companion, you have sacrificed much over the years without complaint," Rajini began softly. "But a wife's duty ends where violation of her inner spirit begins."

Parvathi turned to him with pained eyes. "I knew the day I married you that ours would not be an ordinary life. I was ready to walk through fire beside you. But it terrifies me now to see the same fanatic flame that claimed our Lakshmi, Lakshman, Asha and now threatening to consume Ramu too!"

"Our cause is on the cusp of triumph after long struggle. A free India is finally within sight," Rajini said fervently. "But you are right victory is hollow if it demands martyring our only son."

He clasped Parvathi's hands. "Tomorrow I will inform the movement leadership that my role must now diminish. Our people's dream of independence is larger than one man. My remaining time is owed first to you and Ramu."

Parvathi was stunned to hear this. She realized how anguished her husband must be to even consider abandoning his life's mission so near its apex. "No, I spoke rashly," she said, shaking her head. "I cannot let you turn away from your sacred duty to our nation."

But Rajini silenced her protests, smiling gently. "I fight for a free India where families need never be torn apart by politics or ideology. What use is such emancipation if I cannot protect the family I love most?" He embraced Parvathi warmly. "To care for one's own is the purpose that gives wider service meaning."

In the following days, Rajini spent more time at home, savoring simple moments with his wife and son. Parvathi's lingering pain finally began abating with his sacrificial gesture.

The tale of unequal opportunities:

In a bustling town nestled amidst hills and rivers, Rajini narrated to young Ramu a poignant tale that highlighted the disparities in access to education, showcasing the principle of unequal opportunities that Marx critiqued in his philosophy.

The story revolved around two children, Ravi and Kavi, born in different circumstances within the same town. Ravi came from a wealthy family, residing in a grand mansion adorned with gardens and lavish comforts. In contrast, Kavi hailed from a modest household, a small humble dwelling in a neighborhood where opportunities were scarce.

From an early age, Ravi had access to the finest education. He attended prestigious schools adorned with well-stocked libraries, state-of-the-art laboratories, and skilled teachers. His days were filled with enriching learning experiences, nurturing his talents and broadening his horizons.

On the other hand, Kavi's family struggled to afford his education. The local school, where Kavi studied, lacked resources and proper infrastructure. The classrooms were overcrowded, textbooks were scarce, and the teachers, although dedicated, were overburdened.

Rajini depicted the stark contrast between Ravi and Kavi's educational experiences. While Ravi thrived in an environment conducive to learning, Kavi faced numerous challenges in his pursuit of education. Despite his enthusiasm and intellect, Kavi's potential remained hindered by the limitations imposed by his circumstances.

As the story unfolded, Rajini painted a vivid picture of the hurdles Kavi faced – the lack of adequate resources, the absence of educational support, and the systemic barriers that constrained his aspirations. Despite his determination, Kavi struggled to receive the quality education that Ravi effortlessly enjoyed.

Through this tale, Rajini sensitively conveyed the injustice embedded in unequal opportunities. He emphasized Marx's vision for a society where access to education, a fundamental right, should not be determined by one's socio-economic status or background. Instead, every child deserved an equal chance to learn and grow, irrespective of their circumstances.

As Rajini narrated the poignant tale of unequal opportunities to young Ramu, the story struck a chord within the young boy's inquisitive mind. With eyes wide in curiosity and a heart eager to comprehend, Ramu listened attentively to the story, absorbing its depth and implications.

Ramu's youthful imagination soared as he visualized the contrasting lives of Ravi and Kavi, the protagonists of the story. The vivid descriptions painted by his father brought the narrative to life, evoking empathy and stirring questions in Ramu's thoughtful mind.

As the story concluded, Ramu, intrigued and thoughtful, began to ponder over the nuances embedded in the tale. With a blend of innocence and astuteness, he raised thought-provoking queries that reflected his keen understanding and genuine curiosity.

"Father," Ramu began, his voice filled with wonder, "why couldn't Kavi go to the same school as Ravi? Shouldn't all children have equal chances to learn?"

Rajini, delighted by Ramu's insightful query, embraced the opportunity to delve deeper into the complexities of societal disparities and the principles of equality advocated by Marx's ideology.

"Ah, my dear Ramu," Rajini responded, a sense of pride evident in his gentle smile, "that's an astute observation indeed. You see, in our society, not all families have the same resources or opportunities. Some children, like Ravi, are fortunate to have access to better schools due to their families' wealth, while others, like Kavi, face barriers to quality education due to their circumstances."

Ramu, pondering his father's words, continued, "But why can't everyone have the same schools and teachers? Wouldn't that make things fair for everyone?"

Rajini, impressed by Ramu's insightful question, explained further, "Ideally, every child should indeed have access to good schools and teachers. Marx believed in creating a society where resources, including education, are shared equally among everyone. That way, every child, regardless of their background, would have an equal opportunity to learn and succeed."

Ramu's curiosity continued to spark discussions, his innocent yet profound queries guiding the conversation further. His father, proud of Ramu's inquisitiveness, nurtured his son's curiosity, using these moments as opportunities to impart valuable lessons about social justice, equality, and the ideals of Marx's philosophy.

One evening while reading, Rajini felt Parvathi's intent gaze on him. "What troubles you, my dear?" he inquired.

"I was just reminiscing about the idealistic young man I married, determined to uplift society," Parvathi replied wistfully. "But along the way I lost sight of his humanity amidst the icon he became to the masses."

Rajini chuckled. "Well, that icon was only able to sustain his crusade all these years because you nourished the man behind it - when the world saw only a rebel, you saw your loving husband."

He drew Parvathi into a warm embrace. "After all this struggle, we can finally see dawn approaching for India. But my deepest hope is that our remaining years are filled with the peace and joy that you truly deserve."

As husband and wife sat together quietly, Rajini felt his restless spirit settle into a simple contentment he had long denied himself. He realized that both serving one's country and caring for one's family required sacrifices at times. But neither purpose could be fulfilled fully at the cost of the other. This wisdom calmed the inner turmoil that had been growing in Rajini's heart.

The next morning, cries of "Victory!" awoke the couple. Ramu came rushing in clutching a newspaper - the British had finally agreed to major constitutional reforms after years of civil disobedience! Rajini's eyes misted over. India had taken a momentous leap closer to the freedom he had struggled for all his life. His gaze met Parvathi's, both realizing this was the opportune time for him to return and lead the movement across the finish line.

"There will be unpredictable challenges ahead that require your steady hand," Parvathi said. "But know that I will be beside you as always till the destined dawn." Rajini touched his forehead to hers.

"Then let us complete together what we began all together those years ago - fulfilling the ancient dream of our people. Hand in hand, the couple walked out into the crisp morning. A new chapter in India's freedom struggle beckoned.

Rajini spearheaded the next phase of the independence movement with renewed vigor. The end goal of Purna Swaraj - complete self-rule for India - now seemed attainable.

Chapter 34
Sri Aurobindo - The Vision of Future

At the outset of the early 1900s, the notion of 'Swaraj' as India's ultimate objective in opposing British rule gained prominence. When discussing Swaraj, figures like Bal Gangadhar Tilak and Mahatma Gandhi stand out. Tilak, known as the Lokmanya, vigorously advocated for Swaraj, perceiving it not solely as a political pursuit but as a philosophy encompassing life itself. He famously remarked, "It is a life centered in self and dependent upon self. There is Swaraj in this world as well as in the world hereafter."

For Gandhi, Swaraj extended beyond political freedom to encompass economic and social facets. His vision included Gram Swaraj, emphasizing decentralized power structures.

Sri Aurobindo, another prominent figure in India's Independence Movement, ardently supported Swaraj. In his writings in Bande Mataram (April 1907), he asserted, "We of the new school would not aim for anything less than absolute Swaraj, akin to self-government in the United Kingdom." He firmly believed that aiming lower than Swaraj would demean India's past and compromise its potential.

(In Muthyala nagaram)

The old man said with utmost reverance,* "It is the same Sri Aurobindo from whom Rajini got inspired about agressive nationalism. Along with Marx ideology, Rajini is also inspired and motivated from Sri Aurobindo's ideology and philosophy. Rajini is a rare combination of Marx's communism and Sri Aurobindo's nationalism."

"Please tell us about Sri Aurobindo thatha" curiosly said a student.

The old man nodded and continued...

Born on August 15, 1872, Sri Aurobindo was the third child of Srimati Swarnalata Devi and Krishna Dhan Ghose. Educated in England, he passed the Indian Civil Services exam in 1890 but abstained from the mandatory riding test deliberately. Returning to India in 1893, he transitioned from a revolutionary in the Independence Movement to an ascetic Yogi and Hindu philosopher.

Sri Aurobindo contested the idea that the British would yield power willingly through petitions, advocating instead for organized resistance. He dismissed the efficacy of petitioning and emphasized the need for sacrifice and struggle for freedom.

He urged a vigorous resistance against British authority, believing it was morally justifiable. His conception of Swaraj was rooted in Dharma—a system that acknowledged Western ideals but also recognized a distinct Dharma-based democracy without artificial conflicts.

Central to Sri Aurobindo's Swaraj concept was 'National Education.' He regarded it as the country's most urgent requirement, urging a revamp of the existing education system. National Education, according to him, should encapsulate the legacy of the past, the progress of the present, and the potential of the future.

Wow! Great! Exclaimed a student.

Such a great rishi Sri Aurobindo was said Radhika, a curly hired girl.

The old man nods in agreement and continued the story of Rajini.

"But the decades of agitation had opened rifts between Hindus and Muslims that the British exploited to create sectarian divides. Rajini realized that without closing these chasms, the dream of a united, democratic India would remain unfulfilled even after the British departed. So he embarked on an arduous pilgrimage for Hindu-Muslim unity, up and down the length of the country. At each stop, he preached brotherhood above bigotry through passionate speech and personal example. "

"Hindus and Muslims have coexisted harmoniously in India for centuries as one people," Rajini proclaimed. "Let us not now be divided by the designs of an external oppressor!"

But decades of suspicion and distrust could not be erased easily. Many questioned whether Hindus and Muslims could ever genuinely share the future of an independent India as equals.

To demonstrate the power of faith in each other, Rajini undertook highly publicized fasts and prayers at sacred sites of both religions. Ardent Hindus and Muslims kept vigil by his side as he frailly implored the Almighty for guidance and reconciliation.

These acts of great personal sacrifice finally shook the conscience of communities trapped in cycles of hatred. Slowly, painfully, the walls separating Hindu and Muslim began eroding away.

Young Ramu listened starry-eyed as people praised his Baba's saintly efforts for peace. To Ramu, Rajini's vision of an India embracing all traditions and peoples without bias exemplified the eternal virtues of their land.

But this young man also intuited that the journey from vision to reality would require sacrifices by his generation too.

Rajini smiled upon returning home to hear Ramu speak of carrying forward his unfinished work. "My son, your duty is to build upon our achievements guided by new lights - not just follow the path we charted," Rajini wisely counselled.

This set Ramu pondering deeply about the independent India he wished to see. An India where farmers prospered and children were universally educated. Where women were empowered and the weakest protected. Where rights and laws were the same for all, regardless of religion or caste.

Most of all, Ramu dreamed of an India whose youth were free to reach their full potential, unshackled by colonialism's mental chains. An India that took pride in her ancient values while embracing modernity.

These were the earnest reflections of a young man on the responsibilities he would inherit along with freedom. Though only in his teens, Ramu understood that the struggle's purpose went beyond expelling foreign rulers - it was also to build an equitable nation reflecting timeless ideals of justice.

Rajini saw his own youthful idealism shining once more in Ramu's eyes. But he also sensed his son's generation saw the dawn of independence not as culmination, but fresh beginning. Their vision looked beyond the immediate horizons to the next golden chapter in India's destiny.

This gave Rajini hope that the freedom struggle's gains would be nurtured to full fruition by young Indians like Ramu who embodied courage, compassion and vision.

That night, gazing up at the stars as they had years ago, Rajini shared his own vision with Ramu. "When the British set foot in India centuries ago, they derided us as primitive weaklings. But we persevered and will soon reclaim our destiny. Now we must build an India that is prosperous yet humble, mighty yet magnanimous."

Rajini clasped Ramu's shoulder. "I know our generation will depart satisfied that the future is safe in your hands. Never stop dreaming big for our motherland. Her glory lies ahead of you."

As father and son sat in reflective silence,

Rajini felt the bittersweetness of passing the torch to coming generations. But he knew that true leaders found fulfillment not in power retained, but in inspiring those who came after. For only by uplifting successors could a lasting legacy be forged.

Chapter 35
The Betrayal

As victory neared, tensions erupted within the independence movement over the post-British vision for India. Hardliners demanded immediate social revolution to uplift the oppressed classes. Moderates sought gradual democratic change within existing power structures.

Rajini found himself caught in the middle, trying to balance progressive ideals with pragmatic realities. His singular goal was freeing India through nonviolent civil disobedience. But achieving an equitable society required gradual systematic reforms, not overnight radicalism that could devolve into chaos.

However, the British sought to exploit these divides to undermine the freedom struggle's legitimacy in the final lap. They planted propaganda portraying Rajini as a dangerous militant cozying up to socialist revolutionaries, even as he preached nonviolence publicly.

At the same time, British intelligence agencies contacted disgruntled moderate leaders, urging them to consider political settlements that preserved British strategic interests in free India. They encouraged these moderates to discredit firebrands like Rajini as extremists.

Caught between red-baiting by the British and pressures internally, Rajini felt frustrated and isolated. But he continued steadfastly rallying the masses for nonviolent civil disobedience, the one proven path to Purna Swaraj.

"Why do you still place faith in the elite when they make compromises undermining the struggle's purpose?" a youthful hothead challenged at a rally.

"Without pragmatic unity across groups, our freedom movement cannot represent India's true will," Rajini countered.

"Absolute positions obstruct our larger purpose - wise flexibility is needed in these decisive moments."

But stubborn ideological stands on both extremes continued weakening the movement's cohesion. The British exploited this through propaganda and intelligence manipulation to plant seeds of distrust against Rajini, despite his pioneering role. Matters came to a head when violent protests erupted after moderate leaders backed down on full independence pledges, agreeing instead to dominion status under the British crown.

Rajini urgently tried restoring nonviolent discipline amidst this chaos. But British authorities deceitfully edited his rally speeches to suggest he was instigating the unrest. Before Rajini could rebut this propaganda, he was arrested on fabricated charges of sedition and abetting violence in 1924. As he was hauled away roughly by police, Rajini cried out desperately to the crowds not to betray their principles even in anger.

But truth became a casualty in the ensuing hysteria.

The British launched a vicious crackdown on Rajini's followers to crush the uprising, even as they continued backroom negotiations with moderate elites ready to accommodate them after independence. A misinformation campaign portrayed Rajini as not just an agitator but a conman who had conspired with militants to advance his own power under the guise of nonviolent resistance.

In their isolation, even some independence leaders began doubting Rajini's intentions and methods. Confusion and suspicion reigned, weakening the movement at the pivotal moment. The British had successfully exploited divides to tarnish Rajini and stifle the freedom struggle's surging momentum. Behind prison walls, Rajini was anguished that everything he had devoted his life towards now lay in jeopardy. British propaganda had convinced many that rather than selfless crusader, he was merely a cunning demagogue.

But despite this agony, Rajini felt only hope for India's future. One man's reputation was trivial compared to the cause of independence. Justice would prevail regardless of his personal fate. Rajini clung to this faith fiercely during his isolation. He withdrew into deep meditation and prayer, gathering spiritual reserves to face the tempest brewing outside. The truth would soon emerge victorious, Rajini convinced himself.

Until then, he simply had to endure.

Parvathi wept silent tears hearing the outlandish accusations against her beloved husband. But preserving unity now took priority over even this personal tragedy. Ramu meanwhile seethed with rage at his innocent father's imprisonment. He vowed to fight till Rajini's release. But Parvathi calmed the impassioned youth, counseling that quiet courage would serve the cause better in this dark time. Together, mother and son waited anxiously, hoping redemption still lay ahead for the man whose life embodied the spirit of a nation's struggle.

Rajini languished in prison for months while the independence movement fractured outside. Most moderate leaders now focused on assuming power after the British exited. They left Rajini's reputation ruined to prevent him from posing a challenge. Only a handful still believed Rajini had been framed. But they could not prove his innocence alone.

Meanwhile, brutal suppression continued against ordinary protestors invoking Rajini's teachings.

One stormy night, Rajini was roughly hauled from his cell. British officers perfunctorily handed him a death sentence after a sham trial on treason charges. Rajini simply nodded, bereft more of spirit than life itself after his long isolation. At dawn he would face the noose as a condemned traitor. The British were determined to make an example out of this rebel who had frightened the Empire with his power over the masses.

On March 1, 1924, As Rajini spent his final dark hours in prayer, he thought of Parvathi and Ramu. His heart broke knowing they would have to live with this false stigma. But he hoped the truth would be revealed someday, restoring his family's honor. The next morning, Rajini was marched to the gallows as crowds watched warily. Anti-riot troops stood ready to quell any unrest. The British had turned his execution into a spectacle to intimidate the people.

Rajini scanned the gathered faces silently. Most were passive witnesses detached from this injustice, no longer seeing him as their champion. This pained Rajini more than the death awaiting him. The prison warden offered the customary last chance to share final remarks. Rajini walked slowly to the microphones. He spoke first to the few followers who still stood unwaveringly by his side.

Last Words

"Your steadfast loyalty humbles me. But do not let anger at this injustice push you down the path of violence. Stay true to our ideals - that is how you will redeem my reputation." Rajini then addressed the strategic minds who had orchestrated his downfall. "You may silence me, but you cannot silence the people's longing for freedom. That call will persist till justice prevails."

Finally, Rajini turned to the ambivalent crowds watching his end with detached curiosity. "Friends, they portray me as a traitor to make martyrdom impossible. But in your hearts you know I devoted body and soul to our nation. Preserve that truth till India's destiny is fulfilled." With these final words, Rajini walked calmly up the steps of the gallows. As the noose was tightened around his neck, he closed his eyes and breathed his last with wishing Purna Swaraj for India. His 24 year incredible journey of freedom struggle came to an end. Within moments, the leader who had stirred millions with his revolutionary zeal swayed lifeless before them.

A pall of silence fell over the crowds. Some wept quietly, ashamed at failing this selfless crusader in his hour of need. Others lowered their gaze, conflicted over his true motivations even in death. The British watched closely for any reactions. But the masses remained passive, too broken in spirit to resist anymore. With Rajini gone and the freedom movement fractured, the people simply dispersed quietly. The fire that had raged under this rebel's leadership had finally been extinguished.

Or so it seemed until the following week. During Rajini's funeral, thousands thronged the streets, holding aloft his photo and chanting hymns in his honor. Initially mourning his death, their mood slowly turned defiant.

"Though you took our leader's life, his inspiration lives on!" people roared at British troops monitoring the procession tensely. What began as a solemn honor march became a mass demonstration resurrecting the spirit of defiance Rajini's hanging had sought to kill.

On March 30, 1924, Vaikom Satyagraha (the first ever struggle against apartheid in the World) designed by T K Madhavan and Sree Narayana Guru in Kerala took shape.

Several other Satyagraha activities came into existence, in the light of the baton given by Rajini.

But security forces did not intervene this time.

They realized Rajini's martyrdom had instantly transformed him from dissenter to saint in the people's imagination. Any backlash now risked igniting the passions that had been subdued with his execution. The British had silenced Rajini. But as prophesied, they could not silence the revolutionary legacy he left behind. It continued stirring in the hearts of a people he had awakened, awaiting the day it would once more blaze into freedom's light.

Chapter 36
The Legacy Lives On

In the years after Rajini's execution, India finally attained independence. But it was a bittersweet victory, with the nation divided and thousands dead in communal massacres. Moderate leaders eager to assume power quickly tried burying the memories of fiery revolutionaries like Rajini. They wished to project themselves as the rational mainstream that had delivered freedom through diplomatic negotiations.

But the common people had not forgotten. Across India, villagers continued invoking Rajini's name in their struggles for justice and rights. To them, he symbolized the undying spirit of rebellion against tyranny. In remote hamlets, folk singers glorified the "Immortal martyr" through rousing ballads, keeping his legacy alive in popular memory. Memoir temples were erected in his name, honoring him as a saintly fighter for India's poor and oppressed.

This groundswell of public adulation worried the ruling class. Rajini's strident rejection of imperialism, feudalism and forced hierarchy threatened the order they sought to preserve post independence. His ideals still resonated dangerously among the masses. So textbooks sanitized Rajini's radical activism not even into just one minor aspect of the freedom movement. National histories portrayed him as a sidelined hothead with narrowed visions, denying his pioneering leadership.

These systemic efforts largely succeeded in muting mainstream appraisals of Rajini. Generations born after independence saw him as a fringe fervor rather than the core energizing the struggle. His pioneering movement became a footnote, not central narrative. But this imposed amnesia could not erase the indelible mark Rajini had left as a force of revolutionary change. In the villages and communities where he had awakened dignity and defiance, his words were lore memorized and recited through the years.

"Our Dadaji inspired us to reclaim the lands stolen by thieving zamindars!" aged peasants told their grandchildren. "We are forever in his debt."

"If not for him, we outcasts would still be suffering the inhumanities of untouchability" said lower caste elders. "He made us realize we are children of God, equal to the highest Brahmins."

These inheritors of Rajini's direct legacy knew that textbook histories did not reflect the ground realities. For them, the conquest of independence was not just political - it was socioeconomic emancipation from centuries of exploitation. While national memory slowly buried Rajini's centrality, he remained an immortal crusader in the folklore of the marginalized. Through the generations, stories of his courage and sacrifice inspired many grassroots struggles.

Even within the Reddy family, experiences were mixed. Younger kin found it easier to internalize the moderate narrative and move on from tragedy that had claimed Lakshmi and Rajini. But Ramu, a father himself, made sure his children grew up knowing the true greatness of their grandfather. He refused to let Rajini's martyrdom become just a cautionary tale against radicalism.

"The forces that silenced Baba are the same ones that keep our nation chained to endemic inequity." Ramu told his sons. "We must carry forward his mission in our own way."

This deeper purpose shaped Ramu's career as a journalist and reformer. Through his writings, he resurrected memories of Rajini as a visionary and moral exemplar for modern India during her troubled adolescence.

Slowly, pockets of historians and activists also began re-evaluating Rajini's seminal contributions that had been deliberately minimized. Ramu tried that future generations would finally redeem his revolutionary legacy from the shadows, but could not succeed. Rajini almost won the battle against the white oppressors, but Ramu could not overpower the same coloured oppressors, hypocrites and political bigots.

Though he did what he could to revive the real legacy of the great legend "Rajini Kantha Reddy", which resulted in these kind of statues in some places of Andhra Pradesh, Maharashtra, Orissa and Tamil Nadu.

Saying these words, tears started flowing out of his eyes. He took his saffron robe and wiped them off.

"Thatha, what happened to Parvathi after the incident?" asked a girl.

The oldman replied in a very low voice, "She is gone too with him but after breathing the air of independence."

"What did Ramu do after all his trails?" questioned Sourabh.

"He came back to this village and to their house for the rest of his life", replied the oldman.

" We should let more and more people know about the great man. We have to use all kinds of technology, we will play roleplays, deliver speeches of this Forgotten Hero and create as much as awareness possible" the students started discussing among themselves.

The sun is about to set and the old man got up from his position to go back to the hut.

Right then a girl asked, "What is your name thatha?"

The old man replied "Ramu" as he kept moving.

www.ingramcontent.com/pod-product-compliance
Ingram Content Group UK Ltd.
Pitfield, Milton Keynes, MK11 3LW, UK
UKHW020243240426
12048UKWH00026B/1586